Summer

of Firsts

A richer, fuller
life through
music!

Ann + Paul
Kimpton

Summer of Firsts

As Dale and his friends climbed the steps to the junior high, a tall dark-haired boy stepped in front of them. Dale looked up and said, "Can you tell us where the band room is?"

The boy smirked and looked over at his friends who were leaning against the railing. "Hey, aren't you that hot shot cornet player from Emerson School, the one who saved the town from the fire?" The boy stared down at Dale, his feet planted firmly on the ground, blocking the entrance to the school. "Well, don't think you're coming to my school and taking over. You're on my turf and don't you forget it."

Book Three

SUMMER OF FIRSTS

WORLD WAR II IS ENDING,

BUT THE MUSIC ADVENTURES ARE JUST BEGINNING

PAUL KIMPTON

AND

ANN KACZKOWSKI KIMPTON

GIA Publications, Inc.
Chicago

Summer of Firsts

Paul Kimpton and Ann Kaczkowski Kimpton

Cover art "Valor in the Pacific" by Rober Taylor
Book design, illustration, and layout by Martha Chlipala

GIA Publications, Inc.

7404 S Mason Ave

Chicago IL 60638

www.giamusic.com

G-8495

ISBN: 978-1-57999-972-8

*For our parents who instilled in us a love
of music,
the outdoors,
and adventure*

*For Dr. Carroll Gonzo, our wise GIA editor
For Martha Chlipala for her great illustrations*

For the Adventures in Music Early Readers Club and their suggestions:

Rose Harms and her students in Algona, Iowa.

*A special thanks to the Early Readers Club students Rylee McGuire,
Sammonte Bawden, Jacob Christ Adams, Alex Berhow, Bennita Rose
Geving, Makenna Kathryn Van Zante from Algona, Iowa, for all their
suggestions.*

*Natalie Macleod, Laurie Henshaw and their students at Mountain View
Elementary School in Revelstoke, British Columbia.*

*Eleanor Wilson, Sarah Newton and their students at Mount Begbie
Elementary School in Revelstoke, British Columbia.*

*Yvette Astra, Michelle Gadbois and their students at Arrow Heights
Elementary School in Revelstoke, British Columbia.*

*A special thanks to the Early Readers Club students Jake Leeder, Simon
Blackie, Lauren Channell, Emalyn Adam, Caleb Guenther, Maddy Cole-
Travis, Courtney Atkinson, and from Revelstoke, British Columbia.*

*Thanks to Frank Villella, the archivist for the Rosenthal Archives of the
Chicago Symphony, for the programs and rosters from the Ravinia concerts
on August 11, and 12,1945.*

*A special thanks to Ravinia staff members Amy Schrage and Farah
Ansari for researching the August 1945 concerts and supplying valuable
information on the history of Ravinia.*

*Thanks to the Chicago Symphony and its continuing support of exposing
children to the arts in order to create future generations of musicians.*

SUMMER OF FIRSTS

Chapter 1

FIRST MORNING

Dale lay wide awake as the first rays of sunlight began to filter through his open window. He had hardly slept after all the excitement with his dad's surprise return from the war and Scout's unexpected homecoming. Scout, Dale's beloved Border collie, was sleeping soundly at the foot of his bed, softly panting, his paws moving as if he were running in his dreams. Dale hummed the *Dogs for Defense* anthem as he stroked Scout's fur:

> *From the kennels of the country,*
> *From the homes and firesides too,*
> *We have joined the canine army,*
> *Our nation's work to do;*
> *We serve with men in battle,*
> *And scout through jungles dense;*

We are proud to be enlisted
In the cause of the Dogs for Defense.

Dale smiled as he thought about yesterday. Grandma Rodine, who never did anything spontaneously, organized a backyard party for neighbors, relatives, and even Dale's friends. Within two hours, word had spread throughout Libertyville, and the yard was full of tables, chairs, food, and people celebrating the return of Dale's dad, Jake, and the family's faithful dog, Scout.

The guests wanted to hear why Jake was home from the war in the Pacific. Leaning back in his chair, surrounded by friends and family, Jake explained that the U.S. was slowly winning the war against Japan island by island. He returned home to train other Rangers for a possible invasion of Japan. Dale sat proudly at his father's feet as Jake relayed stories of his four years in battle that would allow other soldiers to learn first-hand what to expect. He was relieved to know his father would be stationed a few hours away, allowing Dad more time to be home before possibly being called for a future invasion.

While Jake continued his war stories, Dale's friends gathered around Scout. P.J.'s dog Smokey ran up eagerly and licked Scout on the nose. Chrissy and Bridget baked a special dog biscuit that Scout gobbled up. Victor, P.J., Karl, Dave, and Tommy wanted to hear about Scout's journey on the train after his escape from the Dogs for Defense training facility in Nebraska. Dale proudly showed his friends the letter from Private Artie Klimza, Scout's handler, that the train conductor had given Jake. On leave, Artie told of finding Scout herding sheep near his Montana home. All wanted to see Scout's ear tattoo, which helped Artie identify Scout. Artie decided the right thing to do would be to return Scout back home via train. Ironically, the train would be the same one Dale's father returned on!

Dale sat up in bed and reached down to pat Scout. He heard a soft knock followed by his father poking his head into the room.

"It looks like you couldn't sleep either," Jake said. "Why don't you and I get some PT before church?"

Dale swung his legs to the edge of the bed. "What's PT?"

"PT is what the military calls physical training. We do it early each morning. After the long train ride and party last night, I need some fresh air and exercise." Jake tossed a green Army Ranger t-shirt to Dale. "Put this on and some gym shoes and meet me downstairs in five minutes."

"*Wow*," Dale thought as he jumped out of bed, "*A real Army Ranger t-shirt*!" In two minutes, Dale was dressed and bounding down the stairs into the kitchen. Dad smiled. "You've learned that to be on time is to be late and to be early is to be on time. Let's get going."

For an hour, father and son ran, did push-ups, sit-ups, and used the beams in the garage as a chin up bar. Dad explained that the military has two types of chin-ups. "The first one is when your palms are facing you. This type is easier and works your biceps more," Dad said as he demonstrated several chin ups.

"We do those in Mr. Cabutti's gym class."

"You mean Mr. Cabutti is still teaching? I had him when I went to school, and I thought he was old back then!" Dad dropped back to the floor of the garage. "The second kind of chin up is called a pull up and it's done with the palms facing away from you. It uses less bicep muscles and more back muscles. It's harder and will take time to master." Effortlessly, Jake jumped up, grabbed the garage beam and pulled himself up and down several times, "I want you to do both kinds each day. Don't worry about how many you do, just do them to exhaustion. Over time, you'll develop stamina."

"What's stamina?" Dale said as he finished doing six chin-ups.

"Stamina means you can keep doing something that takes a lot of effort. It's similar to the word endurance. In the military, we don't lift weights. We run, lift our body weight, and carry our equipment to get in shape. When I'm gone, do these exercises every other day. You're twelve and ready to begin building your body."

Jake rubbed Dale's head, "I've missed being with you and your mom a lot." They walked out of the garage and across the lawn, Jake with his arm around his son's shoulder. Dale could feel the hard muscles of his father's arm. "Come on I smell coffee," Dad said.

Dale's mother was standing at the kitchen sink. Dad quickly walked over to her and wrapped her in his arms. Dale enjoyed seeing his mom and dad together again. Just then, Dale's stomach made a loud, rumbling noise. "Hey, you two lovebirds, after all that exercise, I need to eat."

Mother blushed and said, "OK, let me get my two favorite men some coffee before we have breakfast."

Dad winked at Dale and said, "A full cup?" to which Dale nodded enthusiastically.

Chapter 2

SCOUT'S FIRST SERVICE

Grandma bustled into the kitchen where the family was having breakfast, urging Grandpa to move more quickly so they wouldn't be late for Sunday service. Dale took a bite of a rusk and said, "Is Scout still upstairs in my room?"

"I looked in and Scout was sound asleep in your bed." Grandma frowned; she didn't believe animals should sleep in human's beds. "I heard that dog snoring!" Grandpa stood up so Grandma could adjust his tie. "I think that dog is mighty exhausted from his train ride and last night's party." Grandma cut grandpa off, pointing at the clock saying, "Why don't you all run upstairs and get dressed for church." She winked at dad and said, "I want to leave by 0900 sharp."

Dale ran upstairs to find Scout snuggled under the covers at the end of his bed. Scout lifted his head as Dale rummaged through his closet to find his Sunday clothes. The dog stretched his paws and flopped back onto his other side. "That's OK, boy. I don't blame you for wanting to sleep in." Dale zipped down the stairs to join the family in the living room.

Dale wished he had a picture of the Kingston family walking to church in the warm, March sunlight. Chrissy's family joined them as they passed the Rule's home. Chrissy was in Dale's class, at Emerson School, and both of them played in the school band. Dale played cornet, Chrissy played flute.

Chrissy smiled at Dale as the parents greeted one another. Chrissy's dad shook Dale's father's hand heartily. "Jake, that sure was some party last night." The grown-ups continued talking on their way to the church, leaving Dale and Chrissy to follow a few steps behind.

Dale said, "How's your list coming?"

"I'll have it done for tomorrow's meeting with the gang after school. You said two firsts for the group and the other ten are individual?"

Dad turned. "What list?"

Dale explained how he and his friends had decided to call this summer "The Summer of Firsts," since they were all turning twelve. All of them would make a list of twelve new things that they wanted to do this summer.

"Great idea. Maybe I should start a list of things I'd like to do with you and the family?"

"Even better, you could have two for the family, two for you and me, and the other eight for yourself."

Not to be left out, Dale's mom said, "Don't I get two?"

"OK," Jake said, putting his arm around her. "You can have two also."

Everyone laughed as they continued to church. Pastor Bob, who was waiting on the steps outside the two big wooden doors of the church, waved. He embraced Jake and welcomed him to the Sunday service.

The families followed Pastor Bob and took a seat in the front pew. The organ played the opening hymn, sending chords to the rafters and out through the open doors as everyone sang. Midway through the service, Pastor Bob climbed to the pulpit for his sermon. The words of his booming voice reminded families of the sacrifices everyone must make for the war—no one was exempt. "As spring arrives, we should all consider planting Victory Gardens so we can all do our part for the war effort. No one is too big or too little to get involved."

Just as the pastor's voice increased in volume, he stopped mid sentence, his finger pointed in the air, and froze. The congregation turned to see what he was looking at.

Standing at the end of the center aisle, tilting his head from side-to-side was Scout. The dog hesitated before slowly continuing down the aisle, scanning the pews for a familiar face. Chuckles could be heard throughout the congregation. Dale, stood up to see what was causing the commotion.

Scout was mid-way down the aisle and was sniffing one of the pew legs. Dale had seen Scout do the same type of sniffing at fire hydrants and trees. He turned bright red and whispered loudly, "Scout, Scout," causing Scout to lose interest in that pew. Dale looked up at Pastor Bob, who motioned for Dale to come to the center aisle. He excused himself, squeezed past the Rule family, and stood at the front of the aisle. Seeing his master, Scout bounded the rest of the way down the aisle, jumping into Dale's arms and licking his face. The pastor came up behind Dale and put his hands on the boy's shoulders.

"Scout must have heard me talking about the war effort and wanted to show that even he had volunteered to help." The congregation laughed. "Scout, since you've gotten this far, I say we let you stay for the rest of the service!" To the delight of the parishioners, Scout barked twice in reply.

Scout sat quietly on Dale's lap for the rest of the service. The dog even added a few howls to the final hymn. At the conclusion of the service, the pastor asked Jake, Dale and, of course, Scout to join him on the church steps and greet the departing congregation. On the walk home, the family was particularly quiet until Dale broke the silence. "Scout, I want you to remember that you're still a dog. A special dog, but still a dog."

Dad said, "I'm not sure you'll ever convince Scout he's just a dog. He seems to be enjoying all the attention."

"That reminds me, we should hurry. I put a pot roast in the oven when we left and I don't want it to burn," Grandma said.

As they reached the porch steps, Grandpa said, "I think we need some music. Dale, why don't you get your cornet and play some songs for us while Grandma checks on Sunday dinner?"

"Can I get out of setting the table?"

Grandma frowned, but her eyes were twinkling. "Here we go again with you and Grandpa getting out of your chores because of that cornet. I guess since your dad hasn't heard you play, it will be OK this time." Dale didn't need to hear any more as he took off up the front steps and into the house.

Chapter 3

FIRST MEETING

Dale finished tying his gym shoes just as the alarm he had set the night before went off at zero six hundred. He could smell the coffee percolating in the kitchen. His father must be downstairs. As Dale entered the kitchen, dad, dressed in his green ranger t-shirts, boots, and running shorts, was pouring coffee from the silver pot on the stove.

"Well, look who's dressed for some PT, even on a school day." His dad took a swig from his cup.

"I wouldn't have missed a chance to be with you before you go to Eglin Air Force Base for the week. What time do you leave?"

"This afternoon at fourteen hundred hours."

"I know what that means, two o'clock in the afternoon."

"That's right! Where did you learn to read military time?"

"I learned it from all the orders and telegrams from General Packston over the last few months. I had to know what time to be places, so I could be on time."

Dale's dad laughed and set his coffee down, "If we are going to get our PT in and get you to school on time, let's get going. Where's Scout?"

"I wanted to let him sleep in one more time before he begins joining me each morning."

"Fair enough. Let's start with a short run to warm up," Dad said as the kitchen door shut behind them.

For the next hour, Dale and his father ran up and down Simpson Hill, did sit-ups, chin-ups, pull-ups, and leg lifts. Finally, Dale could hardly do another leg lift.

"Great job, Dale. We've done enough for this morning. I smell bacon and eggs cooking," he said as he put his arm around Dale's shoulder and began walking toward the house. "I want you to promise me you'll take Scout with you every day you work out when I'm gone. I'll feel a lot better about you being alone if you're with Scout."

The table had steaming platters of bacon, eggs, and pancakes. Dale's stomach growled as he slid into his chair. Grandma glanced at Dale and raised her eyebrows as she poured the coffee. "Excuse me," Dale said hastily before grandma could say anything.

Dad gave mom a hug, and continued. "To build a healthy body, you have to exercise and have a well-balanced diet. We just did the exercise, and I can see by the spread on the table that grandma will take care of the diet."

Grandpa asked, "Dale, can you pass the pitcher of orange juice?"

Dale grabbed the pitcher and poured himself a glass first before passing the pitcher to his grandfather.

"Whoa, Dale," his dad remarked. "You just short-stopped the juice!"

Dale looked surprised. "What does short-stopped mean?"

"It means that you were asked to pass something at the table to someone else, and before you did it, you took a portion for yourself. It's not polite and, in the military, it could get you in big trouble."

Dale's face reddened as he looked down at his juice glass. "Sorry, he said sheepishly, almost whispering, I won't do it again."

Dad tousled Dale's hair, "OK, soldier, carry on. Let's eat!"

Dale ate his eggs, bacon, and pancakes with gusto. He leaned back in his chair, enjoying his coffee and listening to grandpa, grandma, and his mom talking about the great weekend they had and then he realized what time it was. "Hey, I almost forgot it's a school day and I have to meet P.J. and Smokey at the fire station. Can I be excused?"

"Yes, you may," Grandma said, "Make sure you take Scout with you. That dog needs to get back to living a dog's life."

Dale put his dishes in the sink and ran up the stairs two at a time. He'd laid out his school clothes, packed his instrument, books, and his list of firsts written the night before so he was dressed and back downstairs in record time.

Dad looked up from his paper. "Don't forget your lunch on the counter. I'll see you on Saturday when I get back." Dale gave dad a hug and was out the door with Scout fast on his heels. It felt good to have the wind in his hair and Scout running along beside him for the first time in over four months. P.J and Smokey were waiting outside the fire station as Dale and Scout rounded the corner onto Main Street. Scout barked and took off running to meet Smokey. When Dale skidded to a stop, the dogs were play wresting as if they had not been apart for months.

"I think Smokey is going to enjoy being tied up with Scout for the day. We don't want to be late to band." They decided to race and make up the lost time. Riding toward Emerson School they could see the gang already heading inside. "Come on, P.J., pick it up! We don't want to be late." Dale was in the lead during the final block.

P.J. stood up to ride extra fast. As Dale pulled into the bike rack, P.J., slammed on his brakes and skidded before crashing into the bike rack. "Wow, would you look at that skid mark!"

"You almost ran me over. I said speed up, not run me over. We'll have to show the gang that great skid mark later."

The boys jumped off their bikes and dashed into the school auditorium to find everyone seated their instruments still in their cases. Mr. Jeffrey was on the podium talking to them. All the students' heads turned as Dale and P.J. flew down the aisle to the stage.

"Sorry we're late Mr. Jeffrey," Dale breathlessly blurted, "but with Scout, and my Dad coming home and a weekend of celebrating, I was running a little late today. It won't happen again," Dale said as he slid into his chair next to Sandra.

"That's OK; we started early so I could explain the audition process for the junior high band next month. I just started, so I don't think you missed anything. As you know, I am Emerson School's band director, and the director of the East Libertyville junior high band, the school you'll be attending next year. Even though I've been your director this year, you must still come to the junior high and play an audition for me. It's very important for you to meet the other band students in grades seven and eight, see the school and, of course, the band room. Going from a grade school to a much larger junior high school that has students from Emerson, Wilson, and Jackson will be quite a change for you." Sandra shifted nervously in her chair. She glanced at Dale who looked calm.

"For the first time, you'll get to play your instruments with older students and compete with them for your chair in the band. I have a philosophy that the best musician, regardless of age or grade, sits in the top chair." Mr. Jeffrey paused and picked up a stack of music and placed it on the table at the front of the room. "At the end of today's rehearsal, please take a packet of audition music. Now, let's start the rehearsal."

For the next hour, the students rehearsed Chrissy's flute solo in Jules Massenet's *Meditation from Thais*. Mr. Jeffrey explained that an arranger takes another composer's music and rewrites the original piece, keeping the basic idea of the song intact. In the case of Chrissy's solo, the original theme was composed for strings but A.A. Harding, director of the University of Illinois bands, arranged it for flute with band accompaniment. The piece could be played either by solo flute or an entire flute section. Mr. Jeffrey decided to have Chrissy play it alone, but today he worked on the band accompaniment. At the end of rehearsal, the students whispered among themselves as they put away their instruments and took the audition music. Bridget leaned over to Chrissy and asked her if she was nervous about going to East. She nodded and added, "but I'm really excited as well."

When all the chairs were almost put away, Mr. Jeffrey said, "Will the brass quintet of Victor, Dale, Sandra, P.J., and Karl stay behind for a few minutes so we can discuss the Sunday Easter service. The rest of you hurry to class, and please tell Mrs. Cooper the others will be along shortly."

Dale said, "Are we really going to get paid for playing in the service?"

Mr. Jeffrey nodded, "But you'll need to work extra hard this week so your performance is worth the money. Can we have a rehearsal today after school?"

The five students looked at each other, waiting for one of them to answer. Finally Sandra said, "I'm sorry Mr. Jeffrey, but we have a meeting planned after school to share our Summer of Firsts lists with each other and decide what our two group events will be. We can't wait to meet, so would it be OK if we practice on Tuesday?"

"What lists are you talking about and what is a Summer of Firsts?"

For the next few minutes, they explained how the idea evolved and how everyone had made a list of twelve new things to accomplish.

P.J. said, "It was my idea to have ten items for ourselves and two that would be for the gang to do together."

Karl cut P.J. off. "Is that how you remember it? Either way, we must have all twelve of them completed between April 1st and the last day of summer before school starts."

Mr. Jeffrey sat back and rubbed his chin. "I'm intrigued by your lists. Of course we can start on Tuesday. I might have to start a list of my own."

On the way back to class, Sandra punched P.J. in the shoulder and said in her best imitation of P.J.'s voice. "It was my idea to have ten items for ourselves and two that would be for the gang to do together."

P.J. turned red, "It was my idea, wasn't it?" Everyone laughed.

Dale said, "Remember, don't get your lists out in class or talk about them. Remember how I got in trouble with Mrs. Cooper the last time I worked on my bugle calls in class? Let's promise."

In unison they said, "Cross my heart and hope to die, stick a needle in my eye."

Chapter 4

GROUND RULES

The rest of the day the gang kept their lists in their desks not wanting to break their promise. As the class read their books during silent reading time, the clock slowly ticked its way toward three o'clock. Finally, Bridget couldn't wait any longer. She leaned forward and whispered to Dale.

"I wish that stupid clock would hurry up! I'm about ready to burst!"

Before Dale could answer, Mrs. Cooper stood up, shot a cross look at Dale and inquired. "Is there something you two want to share with the entire class?"

Dale looked down at his desk, not sure what to say. Mrs. Cooper frowned, standing next to Bridget and Dale's desks. "I hope you two weren't discussing those lists you've made. You both know the rules for silent reading time." Just then, the bell rang and the students began packing up their books.

Dale and Bridget didn't move. Mrs. Cooper's stern face softened, and she waved her hand toward the door. "I think your friends are waiting."

"Sorry Mrs. Cooper," Bridget said. "It was my fault. Dale didn't do anything."

"Bridget, I'm proud of you for confessing. Just make sure breaking the rules doesn't happen again."

Dale looked behind Mrs. Cooper to the classroom door. P.J. held up his list and was pointing at it.

"Mrs. Cooper, how did…."Mrs. Cooper cut Dale off. "Remember, nothing goes on that I don't know about."

Bridget and Dale quickly packed up their books and instruments and bolted for the hallway.

Victor blurted out, "How did Mrs. Cooper find out about the lists?"

P.J. wiped his hand across his brow and stopped suddenly. "Uhmmm… Mrs. Cooper caught me in the coat room looking at my list. I sort of told her about the lists and who was involved." He shifted nervously from one foot to the other.

Victor started to rip into P.J. about violating their agreement, but Dale interrupted. "Alright, the first ground rule for the lists. Don't bring your list to school and talk about it. Period. Now, let's get to the track so we can decide the group events for our Summer of Firsts."

P.J. ran after the group trying to tuck in his shirt that was hanging half way out. "Sorry," he said.

Once they were seated in the bleachers, Bridget began.

"Does everyone have their lists and a pencil?"

Karl nudged Victor. "I may have to borrow one of Bridget's thirty or so pencils from the office supply store she has in her bag."

Bridget rolled her eyes. "Well, at least I'm organized, which is more than you can say."

Dale continued, "OK, second rule. Bridget writes the rules down for us. Agreed?"

"Agreed," they said in unison. Tommy raised his hand.

"Do we have to share our lists? I don't want others to copy me or make fun of mine."

"If we support one another, then we shouldn't feel embarrassed to share them. So rule number three. No one can criticize another person's list. We have to support one another. Agreed?" Everyone nodded their heads.

"And rule number four. You don't have to share your lists until the end of the summer unless you want to. Agreed?"

"Agreed," Bridget wrote the third and fourth rules down.

"I have a question," Dave said. "Can we change our lists once they're made if we come up with a better idea later?"

"Bridget, write this down. Rule number five...you can always make changes, but you must explain why. Agreed?"

"Agreed."

Sandra spoke up. "What if we want to do something with two or three people and not the entire group. Can we count that as an individual one?" Bridget and Chrissy giggled, looking at each other.

"Rule number six. A small group item will count toward your individual list. Agreed?"

"Agreed."

"Now for the group list," Dale said. "Since the brass quintet is getting paid to play the Easter Service this Sunday, I say we take the money and use it for a trip." Dale leaned forward toward the group. "My grandfather can get us cheap tickets to take the train to Chicago. We could go to a concert at Ravinia Park, where the Chicago Symphony plays outdoors during the summer. We could save money by bringing a picnic to eat on the lawn before the concert starts." Dale started talking faster. "This could be our first trip together, kind of a celebration before junior high. It could be a real adventure for all of us." He looked at each of the gang expectantly. "What do you think?"

Chrissy shook her head. "My parents would never let me go to a big city by myself, even with all of you."

"I told Mr. Jeffrey about my idea at lunch time. He said that he would chaperone us."

Karl stood up imitating Dale. "Bridget, write this down. Group item number one. Take a trip to Chicago and Ravinia at the end of summer to hear the Chicago Symphony Orchestra. Agreed?"

Everyone laughed as Dale blushed. "Agreed. But Karl, you just violated rule number four. If we want this to work, we can't make fun of each other."

"Why don't we add rule number seven; no one can take himself too seriously." Karl extended his hand to Dale. "Agreed?"

Dale smiled and shook. "Agreed."

The bleachers began to bounce as P.J. jumped up and down. "Wow, a trip on a train to Chicago all together!"

Dave grabbed the back of P.J.'s un-tucked shirt. "Sit down! You're going knock us off the bleachers."

"I have a group item I'd like to add," Bobby said and stood up. "Let's go to the old abandoned train trestle that crosses Dawson Lake. We could climb out on the trestle under the tracks and fish for carp and bull heads. It would be a fun way to end our summer and share our lists."

Chrissy furrowed her brow and looked at Bridget.

"It's easier to go under the tracks and climb on the supports, than to go out on the tracks and climb down. I've been looking at the trestle for a long time, and I've got it all figured out," Bobby said as he sat down.

No one spoke. Finally, Dale said. "Let's vote. All in favor of fishing from the trestle, raise your hand." One by one, each of the gang raised their hand with Bridget going last.

"Agreed?"

"Agreed."

"Now, Bridget will read us the rules and we'll all copy them down," Dale said.

"And, anyone who didn't bring paper or a pencil can borrow one from the office supply Karl says I have in my bag."

"OK, you got me back," Karl said as he shrugged and accepted a pencil and paper from Bridget.

She cleared her throat and read:

RULES FOR THE SUMMER OF FIRSTS

#1: Don't bring the lists to school and talk about them.

#2: Bridget keeps track of the rules.

#3: No one can criticize another person's list.

#4: Lists do not have to be shared until the end of the summer.

#5: Items can be changed, but there must be a reason for the change.

#6: A small group item can count toward an individual's list.

#7: No one can take him or herself too seriously.

P.J. was madly trying to keep up with the rules. "Slow down. You're reading too fast." Victor glanced over at P.J.'s rules and said, "How can you read that scrawl?"

Bridget tapped her pencil on her notebook to bring the

group back to attention. "Lastly, I would like everyone to write down the two agreed upon group activities."

SUMMER OF FIRSTS GROUP ACTIVITIES

#1: Go on the train to Chicago to attend a symphony concert.

#2: Fish from the Dawson Lake trestle.

When the gang had finished writing down the group activities, Dale said, "Now let's share one item before we end the meeting. Who wants to start?"

Victor jumped up. "I will and I am sure you can all guess what mine is. I want to win one of our races fair and square with no help from you."

Sandra was next. "I've never flown in an airplane, so I put that on my list. I also want to be able to fly the plane."

"Great idea!" Tommy said. "Mine is to swing from a rope on the oak tree at the quarry and jump into the water. I know it's high, but I think I'm old enough and a good enough swimmer."

Dave stood up. "I want to do an Eskimo roll in my kayak without drowning."

"I want to learn to ride a horse," Karl said while he pretended to hold the reins in one hand and whip the horse with the other.

Chrissy said, "I want to play a flute solo with the band at a concert in front of a large crowd."

Bobby went next. "I want to build a soap box race car and race it in the Soap Box Derby."

Dale turned to Bridget and said, "What's on your list?"

"Well, after hearing you kid me about my thirty pencils, I realized I might be a little too organized. I want to do something unplanned..." and she tapped her pencil searching for the right word, "be more... spontaneous. I want to do something without planning every little detail in advance."

"That's so unlike you, Bridget," Chrissy said, giving her friend a hug. "I can't wait to hear what you do."

P. J. was next. "I want to play the string bass so I can be in the junior high jazz band."

Dale was the last to go. He slowly opened his folded list. "I want to learn how to shoot skeet using a shotgun. I watched my dad and Mr. Rule and I'd really like to try it. My dad and grandpa said that when I turned twelve, I could learn, so I'll hold them to it."

The meeting adjourned, and the gang jumped down the bleachers excited to begin planning how to complete the items on their lists.

Chapter 5

BUSY DAY

Dale couldn't stop thinking about the final rehearsal at the church for the Easter service. The cool morning air felt good against his face as he and Scout ran down Simpson Hill. This was Dale's second week of doing PT in the morning, and he was feeling stronger, and he wanted to show his Dad on Sunday how much his strength had improved. He was also anxious about the brass quintet's first performance in public. After descending the hill, Scout slowed down, his tongue hanging out, and he was panting heavily. "Come on, Scout, we're almost done running; you can lie down while I finish the rest of the exercises in the garage."

Scout barked twice and caught back up to Dale as they came to the top of Simpson Hill. Once in the garage, Scout lay on the cool cement floor while Dale finished his chin-ups, sit-ups, pull-ups, jumping jacks, and leg lifts. He heard the screen door slam, and Mom call across the yard, "Don't forget 9:30 on runway 27 Right, the runway that goes next to the big oak tree you and your friends like to sit in. Don't be late; seeing the plane so close will be one unbelievable sight!"

His mom jumped in the Jeep and roared off. All week the gang had talked about seeing their first Boeing B-29 Super Fortress take off from the Air Force base on the outskirts of Libertyville. Dale's mom would be the co-pilot on a new B-29 that had been built in Georgia at the Bell Aircraft Company and was being flown to the West Coast. The B-29 was the first and largest long-range bomber. It could fly over 5800 miles, carry 20,000 pounds of bombs, and could attack mainland Japan. Dale's mom had described the plane's silver exterior, four huge engines, twelve machine guns, and one cannon. It carried a crew of ten and was the first pressurized bomber, able to fly at an altitude of over 31,000 feet. Dale's room was filled with pictures of planes from the two world wars, but the one he liked the best was the B-29.

Dale gulped his breakfast and was out the door for the ride to the Air Force base. He adjusted the rucksack on his back that had his instrument, the Easter music, and his stand, so that he could ride directly to the church after watching his mom take off. As he climbed on his bike, Grandma opened the screen door and called, "Don't forget that tonight we're having fresh, fried fish. Your grandfather hopes to catch some spring blue gill and crappie, but I have a chicken as back up, just in case."

Dale whistled for Scout who wiggled out from under the porch, and the two were on their way. The ride to the base took about ten minutes, and as he rounded the last curve, he slid to a stop. In the oak tree ahead were what looked like six large birds sitting on the limbs. He rubbed his eyes and was ready to send Scout ahead to chase them off when he realized they weren't birds, they were the gang perched on the limbs waiting. Dale laughed to himself and continued the short distance to the tree. From the bottom of the tree, he said, "Hey, you look like crows sitting up there."

The boys started waving their arms, imitating the flapping of wings. P.J. cupped his hands together. "Caw, caw," he said followed by a chorus of crow calls from the rest of the gang.

"We saved your favorite place," P.J. said from the very top of the tree. "I want to get as high as I can, even though it's going to be really loud. I hope we can feel the back wash of the engines as the B-29 flies over us."

From another limb, Tommy said, "Hey, I can see the crew and your mom coming out of the hangar."

Victor shaded his eyes against the early morning sun. "How can you see that far?"

"Easy, I brought the binoculars that General Packston gave us when he rebuilt our fort," Tommy said.

Victor and the other boys peered through their binoculars. "I think Dale's mom is waving at us."

"What's painted on the tail? It looks like the words *Oskee Wow Wow*," P.J. said.

Dale explained as he settled on his favorite branch. "The crew of a plane always gives their plane a name, and then they paint it on the tail or nose of the plane. This plane must have a crew from Illinois because those words are from the University of Illinois fight song. I know that because I went to an Illinois football game where my Dad studied before the war."

"Didn't Mr. Jeffrey tell us that Chrissy's flute solo...what's the name of it?"

"You mean *Meditation from Thais*," Dave said. "Didn't he say it was arranged by the director of the University of Illinois bands?"

Victor, who had a photographic memory, added, "His name is A.A. Harding, and he did lots of arrangements for bands."

"That's where the John Philip Sousa Library and museum is," Bobby said.

"There also was a famous Illinois football player that has a nickname like me: Red Grange, the Galloping Ghost," P.J. called down proudly from the top of the tree.

"Wow!" Bobby said.

"Not wow. You mean Oskee Wow Wow," P.J. said as everyone laughed. They watched through their binoculars as the crew climbed into the plane and Dale's mom gave the boys a thumbs up followed by a salute before climbing in herself. It was several minutes before they saw a puff of smoke from the first of the four engines. One by one, the engines would sputter until finally all four propellers were spinning. Two men ran under the plane and pulled blocks from behind the wheels that had prevented the plane from rolling. Once the blocks were removed, the plane began lumbering down the taxi way to Runway 27 Right, which was directly in front of the boys.

"Look at how big the wings are! They hang over the edge of the runway," Bobby said over the roar of the engines. "How can a plane that big get off the ground?"

"If it doesn't get off the ground, it will run right into us," Dave said.

Dale wasn't worried. "My mom will get it off the ground," he said.

The large silver plane, its glass nose reflecting the sun, slowly turned to face the oak tree. "How come it stopped," P.J. yelled from the top of the tree.

Dale explained what his mother had told him. "All planes stop at the end of the runway before taking off. The pilots talk to the tower to get clearance and do a final check of all the engines and gauges to make sure everything is working correctly. You don't want any part to fail on takeoff. That's when the engines are at full power and there is no room for error."

Dale's voice faded as the engines roared to full power. The nose began to bob up and down as the plane moved down the runway. The engines' high-pitched whine caused Scout and Smokey to bark and run around the tree. The boys had their binoculars up and could see in the large glass nose and cock pit. "Dale, I see your mom!" Tommy said.

The plane was gaining speed as the runway slipped by and Bobby's eyes widened as the plane approached. "Shouldn't it be off the ground by now?" he said nervously.

When the plane was about two hundred yards away, the massive fuselage began to lift off the runway and climb into the air. At the top of the tree, P.J. closed his eyes and ducked as the plane screamed overhead. The wind from the engines blew the limbs back and forth and the boys held fast. The roar of the engines grew softer and softer as the plane climbed higher and higher into the morning light. When the plane was just a speck on the horizon, Dale and his friends scurried down the tree trunk. "That's the most excitement I've ever had," Victor said. Everyone agreed. "I wish I would have put that on my list."

"Can you run these back to the fort for us?" Dale said as he, Karl, Victor and P.J. handed their binoculars to Tommy. "We need to drop the dogs at P.J.'s house before we go to the church for our rehearsal"

"Sure, we'll meet you at the movies after lunch."

The other boys rode off toward the Jungle as Dale, P.J., Karl, and Victor, gathered their belongings. P.J. picked up a large sack with a shiny bell sticking out of the top.

Dale said, "Don't tell me you're going to carry your tuba on your back in that pack?"

"Yep! My mom took an old army duffle bag and added some padding and straps so the tuba doesn't move around. Pretty good idea don't you think?"

Dale shook his head. Karl said, "Wait until Mr. Jeffrey sees you carrying his new tuba on your back. I'd like to know if he thinks it's a good idea."

"I like it. I wish I had one for my French horn," Victor said. "I have to carry mine in one hand and steer with the other hand. Would your mom make a duffle for me?"

P.J. agreed to ask his mom. As P.J. struggled to get his arms through the duffle's straps, Dale reached down to help him. At that same moment, P.J. hoisted the tuba up, and the bell collided with Dale's lips. The force of the impact sent Dale reeling. P.J. turned to see his friend wincing in pain holding both hands to his face.

"It looks like you got in a fight with a tuba, and you lost! I hope you didn't dent my tuba," he said as he wiggled the tuba off his back and examined the bell. After making sure that the instrument wasn't scratched, he looked up to see his friend slowly take his hands away from his lips. P.J. felt badly and apologized.

Dale grimaced as he gently touched his top lip with his fingers. "That really hurt! I hope I'm able to play at the quintet's rehearsal this morning."

P.J. was able to get the tuba back up, this time without help. The boys rode back to town and dropped the dogs off at P.J.'s house. Mrs. Walsh took one look at Dale's face, and offered to wrap some ice in a wash cloth. As they rode to the church for rehearsal, Dale held the cloth with one hand and steered with the other. People on the street would stop and point at the boys, one holding a cloth to his face and one with a tuba sticking out of a duffle bag.

Mr. Jeffrey and Sandra were waiting on the steps of the church as the boys pulled up, his mouth was open in disbelief. First he looked at P.J.

"Is that my brand new tuba on your back?"

"Yes," P.J. said as he swung his leg off the bike. "Isn't it a great idea?"

Mr. Jeffrey didn't answer as he walked around the boy, inspecting the bag and testing the straps. The director shook his head and said, "I have to say you might've invented the world's first tuba bag. Maybe we should patent it?" Then he glanced at Dale, and his face fell as if he had been punched in the stomach. "What happened to you?"

Dale slowly removed the cloth from his face, revealing his swollen top lip. "I accidently hit it on P.J.'s tuba, sir." Mr. Jeffrey frowned and examined his student's face. "I sure hope you'll be able to play," he said as they walked into the sanctuary of the church.

Dale had never been in the church when it was empty, nor had he been in the balcony where the choir sang. Pastor Bob was waiting in the balcony and Mrs. Vincent, the organist, was sitting on the organ bench. She waved at the students who were also in her general music class at Emerson School.

"Welcome, Dale. We're excited to have Emerson's brass quintet play at our Easter service." The pastor stared at Dale's lip, paused, and then went on. "Would you introduce me to the other members of the group?"

"Sure, this is our director, Mr. Jeffrey, who helped get us ready and arranged the hymns and songs we're going to play."

Mr. Jeffrey stepped forward and shook Pastor Bob's hand. "I might have helped them rehearse, but they really practiced hard on their own. I think you'll be very impressed."

Dale then introduced the quintet, and each member stepped forward to shake the pastor's hand. "Sandra plays trumpet, Karl plays trombone, Victor plays French horn and finally...."

Pastor Bob interrupted. "This has to be the famous P.J. I've heard so much about. I recognized you from the ceremony in the park last fall. Let me guess, you play tuba."

P.J. stepped forward to shake Pastor Bob's hand. "How'd you know that?"

Pastor Bob smiled. "It might be that you have a huge tuba on your back."

The group laughed, and they began to relax as the pastor handed everyone a program. "Your songs appear in the program so you know when to play. I've also put your names in."

P.J. flipped the pages of his program. "Pastor Bob, I don't see my name in the program."

The pastor scanned the names. "I don't understand. Isn't your name Charlie Walsh?"

P.J. turned bright red. "Oh, I'm sorry. I haven't heard anything but my nickname for the past six months, so I was looking for P.J."

Everyone laughed as they followed Pastor Bob to the room off the balcony where they would store the cases and warm-up on Sunday. "We'll have some food and drink for you before the service."

Karl took his trombone out of the case. "Wow, we're not only getting paid, but we're getting food, drinks, and our own room. I feel like a real professional."

Dale nodded. "Let's just make sure we play like it." He gently ran his tongue across his top lip, brought his cornet up, but decided against playing a note.

The quintet set up their stands in the balcony and adjusted their music. In addition to the hymns they would play with the organ, they would perform five numbers by themselves, two at the beginning of the service as the congregation entered, one during the offering and finally two at the end of the service as everyone was leaving.

Mrs. Vincent played the first chord, which flooded the church with a beautiful sound that engulfed the rafters. The quintet began to play but Victor put his horn down and stared open-mouthed at the ceiling.

"What's wrong Victor?" Mr. Jeffrey asked?

"Nothing, but is that really us playing? I've never heard such sounds before."

"When you play in a church with high ceilings, marble floors and walls, your sound spreads out and fills up the room. It's not like our auditorium with low ceilings and big curtains that dampen and absorb the sound."

It was time to continue rehearsal so Dale nodded his head and the quintet began to play. Dale had trouble getting out the first note, and the group stopped. Sandra leaned over to Dale and said, "Just relax, you'll be fine." The first piece went OK until Dale had to play a high G. After several attempts, Mr. Jeffrey said, "Dale, give that lip a rest. You'll be able to hit it tomorrow."

For the most part, the quintet played well, and Pastor Bob said. "If you play like that tomorrow, you'll definitely have earned your money."

"Pastor Bob, we aren't going to play like that tomorrow," Dale said emphatically.

Pastor Bob tilted his head. "What do you mean?"

"We're going to play even better." Dale said confidently and he meant it.

The group packed up their instruments and headed down the steps of the church. Dale turned to Sandra. "I'm sorry I let you down today. I promise I'll do better tomorrow."

Sandra touched Dale gently on the shoulder, and he looked into her light gray eyes. "I know how much this performance means to you. You'll be able to do it." Her pony tail flipped as she turned down the sidewalk. "See you later at the movies."

As they slid to a stop outside of P.J.'s house, the dogs, tails swishing rapidly, were patiently but anxiously waiting. Karl helped P.J. off with his tuba before he could get off his bike, "I don't want Dale getting anywhere near this tuba."

As they entered the kitchen, the boys were greeted by Mrs. Walsh. "Wash your hands and come to the table. I have sandwiches ready." She looked closely at Dale's lip which had ballooned to twice its normal size. "Let me refresh that ice before you go to the movies."

Chapter 6

NEWS FROM THE WAR

When lunch was finished the boys were so full they decided to take their time riding to the movies. The early afternoon sunshine filtered through the emerging leaves of the overhanging trees, creating dappled patterns on the lawns.

"I almost forgot what it was like not to race," Karl said as he swerved back and forth from one curb to the other.

"Look up ahead. Isn't that Chrissy, Bridget, and Sandra walking on the sidewalk?" Victor said.

"What do you say we sneak up on them and scare them?" Dale got Karl's and P.J.'s attention and used the hand signals they used in the Jungle to signal a plan. P.J. would ride slowly past the girls on the street as a distraction while Dale, Karl, and Victor raced down the sidewalk and slammed on their brakes behind them.

P.J. slowly rode ahead, pretending not to see the girls.

"Hi P.J." Bridget said.

Chrissy and Sandra shouted, "Hey where's the rest of the gang?" P.J. ignored them and continued riding. The girls followed his movements wondering why P.J. ignored them.

Sandra was about to call his name when skidding tires on concrete filled the air behind them. All of the girls screamed and jumped off the sidewalk just as Victor yelled, "Look out!"

P.J. turned around, laughing, and rode over to the girls. "Wow, those are swell skid marks!"

Chrissy, fire in her eyes, said crossly, "That was mean! You scared us half to death!"

Her anger disappeared when she noticed Dale's lip. "What happened to your mouth?"

Bridget went up to Dale and gently brushed his lip with her finger. Speaking with a tightness in her voice she wondered out loud, "Aren't you playing at the Easter service tomorrow?"

"I'll be OK. But you have to admit that you were totally not paying attention. Remember to always be aware of your surroundings."

Karl nudged Victor, "Yeah, Dale, just like you were aware of P.J.'s tuba."

"You got me on that one, Karl. Come on, ladies, hop on and we'll give you a ride to the theatre. Victor, you take Sandra, Karl you take Bridget, and I'll take Chrissy."

"What about me?" P.J. said.

"Sorry, we're all out of girls, and you're probably tired

from carrying that tuba all morning. Let's go, I don't want to be late."

Bobby, Tommy, and Dave, who were waiting outside the theater, waved for them to join them in the ticket line.

"We were worried you were going to be late," Dave said as the line began to move.

"We would have been if the boys had not given us rides," Chrissy said punching Dale in the shoulder.

"Sorry about scaring you, but at least you're here. I can't wait to see *Tarzan and the Amazons.*"

Bobby leaned over and began to swing his arms like a chimpanzee, imitating a chimp sound, "Ooh, ooh, ooh, eee, eee, eee, aah, aah, aah!"

Bridget laughed and reached down and held his hand like Tarzan would and said, "Come on Cheetah, we don't want to hold up the line."

"Ooh ooh ooh eee eee eee aah aah aah," he said as they entered the theatre.

The boys filed into a row in the middle and the girls sat in front of them.

"I am looking forward to the newsreel today," Dave said, "Last night on the radio I heard that the war against Japan and against Germany are really turning in our favor and could end soon."

Sandra turned around, "My dad says we have a long way to go since both Japan and Germany will really stand and fight when we get close to their home land."

The entire nation had been glued to the radio since the Battle of the Bulge in December and the rescue of the city of Bastogne by General George Patton. The war had gradually started turning in favor of the Allies. Dale was especially interested in the war in the Pacific because that's where his father had been fighting. Each night he lay on the living room carpet listening intently to news of the battle of Iwo Jima, the bombing of mainland Japan, and General MacArthur taking back the Philippines and Corregidor. He would never forget how MacArthur said, "I shall return" when he had to evacuate the island in 1942.

Dale's thoughts were interrupted when the curtain opened and the lights dimmed, causing everyone to quiet down. The light from the projector flickered on the screen and the newsreel began with the announcer saying, "The war against Germany rages on with the Allied forces racing across Europe like a juggernaut. After fierce fighting in Cologne, Germany, the Allies have finally captured the bridge at Remagen. Now we have a bridge and a route into the heart of Germany."

The screen suddenly showed a squadron of B-29's taking off from a runway in Burma.

Tommy jumped up, "That's just like the plane we saw this morning!"

"Shh, you're going to get us in trouble," Dave said pulling Tommy back into his seat.

The announcer continued, "Elsewhere in the Pacific, a squadron of B-29s is taking off to fly over four thousand miles to lay mines that will disrupt Japan's shipping. These brave men risk their lives flying missions every day trying to bring this war to an end."

The newsreel continued but Dale's thoughts turned to his dad who was training soldiers for the final assault on the Japanese homeland and how dangerous it would be if he had to go back. Dale felt a punch in the shoulder and turned to P.J.

"What was that for?"

"The main movie is starting and you weren't paying attention. I didn't want you to miss out."

The movie told the story of how Tarzan, the jungle man, helped defend a tribe of Amazon women from some evil archeologists who wanted to steal the tribe's riches. Tarzan uses his famous jungle call "Ah-ah-AHHHH, ah AHH, ahahahahahhhhh" to alert the animals of the jungle and save the Amazon women.

When the movie ended, the entire audience was either imitating the Cheetah sound or Tarzan's jungle call.

As the group filed down the aisle, Sandra said, "I wish I could live in the jungle."

Tommy disagreed. "You wouldn't last five minutes with all those bugs, snakes, lizards, and spiders. I've seen how you act when you see a spider and it's not pretty. Plus, I don't think your mom would let you wear those jungle outfits."

"I would like a pet chimpanzee."

Bobby leaned against Sandra's shoulder, "You do? Ooh, ooh, ooh, eee, eee, eee, aah, aah, aah!"

"Come on Cheetah. I am starved for dinner," Sandra said taking Bobby's hand and leading him out of the theatre.

Once outside, Dale said, "Do you think we'll win the two wars? I'm worried about my dad and everyone who is still fighting overseas." Everyone was silent but gave Dale a reassuring look and Chrissy touched him lightly on the arm.

"The next several months will be the turning point and the end should come soon," Victor said confidently. "For now, let's concentrate on our Easter performance tomorrow and earning some money for our trip to Ravinia. Hope your lip feels better, Dale."

The girls walked home, and Dale rode to P.J.'s house to get his horn and Scout before heading home. As he climbed Simpson Hill, he kept thinking about the war and his dad. By the time he reached the crest, Dale realized he might as well enjoy the time he had with his dad now rather than worry about the war. Grandpa and dad were waiting on the porch and Scout took off for a scratching from grandpa. His dad stood up to greet him, but Dale quickly turned his head down to hide the hot tears that had welled up in his eyes.

His dad put his hand on Dale's chin and lifted it up, closely examining his face. "Did you get in a fight?" not seeing Dale's moist eyes.

"Yes, but it was with a tuba."

Dale's father relaxed, chuckled, and he tousled Dale's hair. "I hope that tuba isn't as messed up as your face!"

Just then grandma called from inside the kitchen, "Looks like the old man and the sea came through this time. Dinner's served."

"Give a man a fish and you feed him for a day. Teach a man to fish and you feed him for a lifetime," grandpa said as he opened the door.

At dinner, Dale told the story of the tuba run-in, the Easter rehearsal, and the new Tarzan movie. "Is all the news about the war true? Will it really be over soon?"

"I think if luck is on our side, we'll see both the war in Europe and the one in Japan end soon."

"Enough war talk," grandma said, "Why don't you excuse yourself and go lay out your clothes for tomorrow and shine up your cornet. Here's some more ice for your lip."

Dad said, "Do you know that this will be the first performance of yours I will hear?"

Those words reminded Dale that he hadn't been able to reach any of the high notes at the rehearsal. "I hope I make you proud."

Chapter 7

EASTER—APRIL I, 1945

Dale woke with his head full of music, fingerings, and a thicket of notes. Mr. Jeffrey told the group that if you can sing your part, you can play it. Last night, Dale decided to rest his lips and instead finger the notes and sing the parts rather than play them. In the morning, his cornet case was still open and his music was on the wire music stand next to his bed. His black pants, pressed white shirt, and red tie with the embroidered cornet were neatly folded on the chair. For good luck, Dale vowed to wear the tie that Bridget had given him for Christmas. Once he was satisfied that he was ready for the Easter service, he changed into his ranger t-shirt and running pants and set his gym shoes by the end of his bed so he would be ready for his early morning P.T. with his dad. His thoughts were interrupted with a soft knocking on the door.

Dale jumped out of bed, grabbed his shoes, and rapidly opened the door. "Well look who's ready. Let's get some exercise before your big performance. A little physical exertion will help clear your head," Dale's dad said as he headed down to the kitchen to go outside.

"Why don't you lead the exercises, so I can see how you've improved. I hope I can keep up!"

"Follow me!" Dale took off running, toward Simpson Hill. He dashed up and down Simpson Hill twice, adding a short, vigorous sprint to challenge his dad who seemed to be sweating a little more than usual. Once back at the garage, they each took turns doing chin-ups and pull-ups on the garage beams and finished with sit-ups and push-ups.

Dad wiped the sweat from his forehead. "You've really improved over the last week. If you keep this up, you'll be in great shape."

"I've worked out each day like you asked and Scout runs with me each day. I think he seems stronger too."

But, before Dad could answer, they heard the growl of an engine and the squeal of tires on the street. Dale's mom roared up the drive way in a green Army Jeep with the top off. She slammed on the brakes coming to a stop next to the two sweaty figures in the garage.

"I made it!" she said jumping out of the driver's seat and giving them both a hug. "We flew all night from San Diego after delivering the B-29 and we just landed. I didn't want to miss out on the big performance today." Just then, she glanced at Dale and wrinkled her brow. She opened her mouth to say something, but Dad interrupted. "I need some breakfast," and he grabbed her by the hand.

In the kitchen, the smell of freshly brewed coffee and frying sausages greeted the trio. Grandma stirred a big skillet of scrambled eggs.

The conversation during breakfast was fast paced. Grandpa boasted about his successful fishing trip and Dale's mom enthralled the family with her cross country flight to San Diego in a B-29 without having to stop for fuel. No one, however, mentioned Dale's still swollen lip or the fact that he had only eaten a spoonful of eggs. Finally grandma looked at the clock. "Don't you think you should get ready?" Dale took one last sip of coffee and stood up.

"Be sure to tie up Scout before you leave. I don't think Pastor Bob will want his service interrupted again."

It took Dale several tries before he got his tie tied right. He stared at himself in the mirror, carefully examining his lips. The swelling had gone down, but his top lip was still tender. He grabbed his cornet, stand, and music and headed back down stairs.

As he entered the kitchen, his dad was the first to speak. "Did you tie that tie all by yourself?"

Dale nodded.

"I think you're growing up into a fine young man and a great musician," Dad said as he stood up and patted Dale on the back. "I know you'll play your heart out today, son."

Dale rode his bike to the church and as he pulled up, the members of the quintet were sitting on the steps. He looked first at Karl, then Charlie, then Victor and finally Sandra. They all had on white shirts with red ties just like Dale, and each one had an instrument embroidered on the front.

"What do you think of our ties?" P.J. said "We decided that if we're going to play together through high school, we needed a uniform."

Dale examined the intricate French horn on Victor's tie. "I think it's a great idea. Where'd you get 'em?"

"My grandma did the embroidery," P.J. said, proudly waving his tie with a tuba as they climbed the steps to the church doors.

Pastor Bob stood in the foyer with a welcoming look and he smiled. "You sure look spiffy! I love your red ties"

White lilies adorned the altar of the church and at the end of each pew there hung a large, white bow. "The church looks great," Victor said as they climbed the stairs to the balcony.

Charlie raced ahead and was the first in the room. "Look at all the food," he said stuffing a blueberry muffin in his mouth.

"I'm glad you like it. Just be sure you're ready by 9:45 sharp," and the pastor left to prepare for the service.

Sandra noticed Dale hadn't touched any of the food. She squeezed his hand. "Why don't I play the first part and you can play my lower part." Dale stiffened. There was no way that he would let Sandra play his part. "Thanks, but I'm going to do this," he retorted with an air of confidence.

As Charlie took the last muffin, Mr. Jeffrey entered the room. He looked admiringly at his students.

"You look just great with the matching ties! I wish I had one."

"Just a minute," Sandra said as she went to open her case. "You didn't think we would let the leader of the group go without a tie. We had a baton embroidered on it, especially for you."

Mr. Jeffrey brightened, held up the tie, and said in a delighted tone, "It's beautiful!"

By the time Mr. Jeffrey had finished tying his tie, the quintet was seated in the balcony with a heightened sense of excitement and anticipation.

"Today I want you to tune to the organ so we all match pitch. We can't tune the organ, so we must tune to it." First the quintet played long tones and lip slurs on their mouthpieces followed by scales in the keys that matched the music they would be playing. Dale lightly touched the mouthpiece to his lips and buzzed. His top lip still felt a bit numb, but he was able to play the low tones.

"I think we're ready to tune. Mrs. Vincent, will you play a Concert Bb for us?" As she played the note, each student played and made adjustments to their horns so they matched pitch. When it was Dale's turn, at first he played a low C. The note was solid and full. With renewed hope, he played the C on the staff. This time he bobbled the note before hitting it. He turned red, and Mr. Jeffrey gently said, "Just remember to hear the note before you play."

"Can we play a few bars of the first song so we can hear how we sound before the congregation arrives?" Victor said. "I want to hear the sound again so I don't stop playing like I did the last time."

The director held up his baton, gave two beats in tempo, and the quintet began to play, filling the sanctuary with wonderful instrumental music. The sound was rich and full. After several lines of music Mr. Jeffrey signaled a cut off. With an enthusiastic look, he glowingly said, "You're ready. Now, get a glass of water to have by your chair. Sometimes your mouth gets dry during a long service."

After getting the water, Charlie called them over to the window overlooking the front steps of the church. "Look at all the people waiting to get in. I've never seen so many people!" Dale quickly went back to his seat and nervously took a gulp of water.

"It's almost time to start." Mr. Jeffrey said, glancing at his watch.

From the front of the church, Pastor Bob's voice boomed. "I'm going to let the congregation in. Begin when you see the first person enter."

Mrs. Vincent smiled and said to her students, "Good luck! You'll be great."

The quintet looked at each other and smiled, giving each other a thumbs-up. The first person they saw was Chrissy who had on a blue flowered dress and matching hat. She waved excitedly at her friends in the balcony. Dale flushed and quickly looked away so he wouldn't be reminded of the people who had come to hear them play.

Karl stood up and waved his trombone. Mr. Jeffrey said sternly, "We never wave to the audience when performing." He picked up his baton and raised his arms.

The first selection was Fauré's *Pavane*. The piece was slow and lyrical and showcased the students' ability to balance and blend. Dale was able to play all the notes and the last chord slowly diminished until it disappeared. As the service continued, Dale's hands felt sweaty against the brass of his instrument. He couldn't stop thinking about the final piece, *The Rejoicing*, by Handel, which was one of the quintet's favorites. It was also the hardest. Mr. Jeffrey had selected the piece because of the triumphant sound and running eighth and sixteenth notes. Dale would need every ounce of concentration to hit the high notes, especially the final chord. He wasn't able to play the note yesterday. *Would the last note the congregation hear be the wrong one?*

Dale fingered the notes as he sat waiting for the concluding number. He took deep breaths to calm himself down. *I can do this.*

At last Mr. Jeffrey cued the group to bring up their instruments. *This is it.*

Mr. Jeffrey lifted his baton, gave the down beat, and the group began. The notes sounded strong, sure, and punctuated the air with musical grandeur. The final chord soared through the rafters of the church with the high G from Dale's cornet piercing the top. As the notes hung in the air, the quintet brought their instruments to their laps. Spontaneously, the congregation broke into applause. Mr. Jeffrey asked the group to stand and bow showing their appreciation for the applause. Dale looked down to where his family was sitting and saw his dad proudly turn around and smile. He had made his family feel proud. Eyes sparkling, Chrissy was applauding with great enthusiasm.

Once the group sat down and the applause died away, Pastor Bob continued in a solemn voice, "This morning a large amphibious assault was launched on the island of Okinawa. This strategic island is only 350 miles from the island of Japan. Let's pray for these brave men fighting in the Pacific. I encourage you to go home and listen for further information about this battle on this historic Easter Sunday."

The congregation sat in silence before whispered conversations began. Pastor Bob motioned for Mrs. Vincent to play as the congregation slowly filed out, speaking in hushed tones.

When the church was empty, the quintet gingerly packed up their instruments and went outside. The sun was warm on this first day of April and Dale's family was outside eagerly waiting for him.

"That was the most beautiful music I have ever heard," his father said shaking his Dale's hand with a firm grip. Dale's mom started to say something when Chrissy burst through the crowd. She gave Dale a big hug. "That was amazing. You were so good," and Dale felt his heart beat speed up, he blushed and before he could answer, she ran over to Sandra who was standing with her family.

The congregation continued to congratulate the musicians until grandma said, "I'm going home to check on the pot roast and turn on the radio. You come along when you're ready."

Grandpa, mom, and dad turned to leave. Mom said, "Dale, come home when you're ready."

"I'm hungry, so I won't be long."

After everyone had left, the quintet lingered on the church steps in the warm late morning sun congratulating themselves on a successful performance. Pastor Bob stopped by the group. From his pocket he took out a large envelope and handed it to Dale. "I want to thank you for your beautiful playing today. It was truly magnificent and something the congregation will not forget. I hope I can hire you all again."

The quintet responded in unison with thank you and Victor blurted out, "We're going to use the money to go on the train to Ravinia to hear a concert this summer." Pastor Bob gave the group an approving look and remarked that using the money to go to a professional concert was a splendid idea. "I love going to Ravinia and hearing great music outside. Now I'm going home so I can listen to the news of the war on the radio," he said as he went back into the church.

As the group walked to the bike rack, P.J. said, "I can't think of a bunch of better friends than you guys, and that means you too, Sandra," to which she smiled broadly. "I hope we keep doing stuff together and playing together. Agreed?"

"Agreed," they said, and they pedaled off in different directions. As Dale slowly and pensively rode his bike up the hill, his thoughts turned to the war news that Pastor Bob had announced. The war with Japan was accelerating, Dale worried, *would his dad be called back into action and return to the Pacific?*

Chapter 8

A DAY TO REMEMBER, APRIL 12, 1945

As Dale rode to the fire house to pick up P.J., he could not believe that it had been almost two weeks since the quintet had performed at the Easter Service and the assault on Okinawa had begun. Each night his mom, grandfather, and grandmother would sit in front of the radio and listen to the progress of the war in Japan and in Europe. Dale was particularly interested in the news from the Pacific, since his dad was training new soldiers for the invasion of Japan. Dad had been right about the Japanese putting up a tough fight as they began defending their homeland. The battle for Okinawa was very intense and extremely costly in American and civilian lives. Dale constantly worried that soon his dad would return to continue the fight in the Pacific. Scout barked twice, clearing Dale's mind of all the war thoughts when he spied Smokey and P.J. loafing at the curb outside the firehouse. Scout bounded forward in a fast trot and Dale pedaled faster to keep up.

P.J. jumped up from the curb as Dale raced toward him. Just as he got out of the way, Dale slammed on his brakes hard, leaving another long, black tire mark on the street. "Hey P.J.," Dale said jumping off his bike. "Looks like you anticipated my skid this time instead of whining that I almost ran you over like you usually do."

"One of these days you're going to crash that bike into the curb, if you keep skidding like that."

"You have to admit that is another great skid. Look, I count nine skids on the pavement. I hope it doesn't rain for a while. I like seeing if I can beat the old ones," Dale said as he walked Scout to the back of the firehouse to be tied up for the day with Smokey.

P.J. ran and hopped on his bike. "Let's hurry! I finally learned all of my parts and today we will play straight through each piece. Sometimes I get tired of stopping and starting all the time in rehearsal, it is really frustrating."

"Me too, but if Mr. Jeffrey doesn't stop and correct what we're doing wrong, then how'll we fix the mistakes and make the group better?"

P.J. thought about what Dale said. "You might be right, but it's still annoying, however, I do like playing without stopping. Come on... I'll race ya," he said getting a head start on Dale.

Dale knew he could catch P.J. His legs were getting stronger each day, since he started doing the P.T. each morning. In less than a half a block, Dale had caught P.J. and raced ahead. As he flew by P.J., he thought, "If I'm this strong after only three weeks, what will I be like by the end of the summer." His thoughts were interrupted when he heard the gang shouting as they waited at the school bike rack.

"Come on P.J. Don't give up! You're only a block behind!" Dave gleefully observed as Dale slid to a stop.

"That's not fair, Dale! You cheated somehow!"

"I didn't cheat. I'm getting stronger from exercising each morning. You should try it."

P.J. didn't get a chance to answer as Chrissy, Bridget, and Sandra ran by and shouted, "Race you to the auditorium!"

Victor watched in admiration. "Did you see how fast they were running? If they're getting faster, I'll never win a race this year and my list won't get finished." Victor whipped around and took off running after the girls.

"I'll bet we can catch them!" Bobby said leading the chase after the girls.

The girls were already inside looking very self-satisfied by the time the boys ran down the aisle of the auditorium. Everyone began setting up and warming up their instruments until Mr. Jeffrey stepped on the podium, which was the signal to stop playing and talking. "We're only two weeks away from our final concert of the year. I want to spend as much time as possible rehearsing. Let's begin by warming up on *Chorale Number Seven*."

The band enjoyed playing chorales. They were not very hard note wise, but they were challenging in the need for good breath control and appropriate, phrasing, tempo, dynamics, and most important of all, watching Mr. Jeffrey's baton. He had explained that when he conducted a chorale, he would slow down some phrases and speed up others to give the music emotional intensity that would build toward the ending chord.

When Mr. Jeffrey gave the cut-off at the end, he said, "Can anyone tell me if the last chord was major or minor?"

He waited a few moments to give the students a chance to think. Mr. Jeffrey believed that everyone was responsible for answering the question, and he liked to select the student that did not raise his or her hand.

P.J. raised his hand, waving it back and forth.

"P.J., you know I don't like you trying to get my attention by waving your arms, but since I've not called on you to answer a question for quite some time, you can answer."

P.J. stood up and rested his tuba on the chair. "This is easy. First, the chord sounds sad or dark, which you said is a clue that it is minor. If it sounded open or happy it would mean it is major."

"How I really knew it was minor was that the key of the chorale is E-flat major and the ending note of the choral should be E-flat for me, since I play the bass part, but it isn't. The last note for me is a C.

If a song ends on the sixth note of the scale or a third below the concert key, it's usually minor."

"You're absolutely correct. Now, how about a question to the percussion section? Dave, tell us which minor scale the choral is based upon. Is the scale natural, harmonic, or melodic minor?"

Dave swallowed and picked up his mallets. "It's easier for me to play the different scales on my marimba so I can hear the notes."

"OK, go ahead."

"You told us that music is rarely written in natural minor, which uses the same key as the major but starts on the sixth note of the concert scale or a third lower than the concert key.

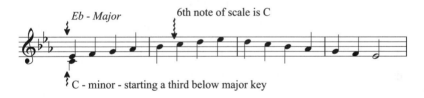

Like P.J. said, the concert key is E-flat, but the song is minor so the key would be C minor. The natural minor scale would use all the same notes as E-flat but start and end on C. Let me show you."

Dave played the scale up and down on the marimba. Mr. Jeffrey encouraged him to continue the explanation.

"You also told us that a melodic minor scale is just like the natural minor, but the sixth and seventh notes are raised going up the scale. Coming back down, those notes return to the natural minor scale. I think you said it sounds like a melody or goes up one way and comes down a different way." Dave took his mallets and demonstrated the scale.

"But how do you know that this song isn't in melodic minor?" Mr. Jeffrey said.

"Sorry, I forgot to tell you why. In my music, I don't have any A naturals. I just have B naturals throughout the entire song. I also don't have any B-flats that would show up when the melody went down in the natural minor scale." Before Mr. Jeffrey could answer, Dave said, "I think it is in harmonic minor, which is my favorite. The harmonic minor starts on C again and has only a raised seventh note that is a B natural going both up and down. The scale sounds like the music played in the movies when a genie comes out of a bottle or when a snake charmer charms a snake."

Dave played the scale. When he finished, he went back and played the last four notes of the scale back and forth really fast.

Dave looked up and said. "Not a bad answer coming from a drummer, right Mr. Jeffrey?"

Mr. Jeffrey grinned and answered, "Today you earned the title of percussionist. Let's all play the C-harmonic minor scale and the chorale one last time."

When the choral ended, Mr. Jeffrey had the students put their music in concert order. "I'll read each selection and once you have them in order, put them on the left side of your folder. The rest of the music should be on the right."

When they had finished putting the music in order, the band played through the opening march *Amparito Roca* by Jaime Teixidor. After several corrections, Mr. Jeffrey turned to Chrissy. "When we finish this piece, I want you to go off stage and wait for your solo. You can get a drink of water and have some time to rest before coming out. The second selection will be *Concert Overture* by Robert G. Johnson. Today let's skip the second number and spend the rest of the rehearsal working on Chrissy's solo, *Meditation from Thais.*"

Bobby, the first chair clarinet, blurted out, "Oskee wow wow!" in reference to the arranger being the University of Illinois band director. He quickly cupped his hand over his mouth once he realized what he had done.

All eyes were on Bobby. Slowly taking his hands off his mouth, he looked up at Mr. Jeffrey. "Sorry! I was excited when you mentioned the piece. On Saturday, we watched Dale's mom take off in a B-29 with *Oskee Wow Wow* painted on the tail. Dale told us that the expression was part of the University of Illinois fight song."

Mr. Jeffrey laughed. "I'm not mad. In fact, I'm impressed that you put together the name of the plane with the arranger of Chrissy's piece and the University of Illinois."

"Let's get back to work on the solo. Chrissy, will you play the opening phrase?"

Chrissy put the flute to her mouth and took a deep breath. What followed was the most beautiful sound Dale had ever heard.

The sound was warm and round. Dale knew she had been working on her tone and putting expression and emotion into her playing. Night after night, he could hear the notes of the piece drifting out of her bedroom window.

When she finished playing the first phrase, the entire band began pounding their feet on the stage in appreciation of her hard work. They had only done that once before when Mr. Jeffrey had come on stage for their first concert. Clapping alone would not have been enough.

Chrissy blushed and bowed slightly to her friends before turning to Mr. Jeffrey. "What do you think? Have I found the emotion and expression you said I needed to play this piece?"

"Not only that, but your tone is amazing. What did you do?"

"I did three things. First, you said tone is everything, so I relaxed my embouchure or lips like you suggested. I also played long tones, arpeggios, and breathing exercises. Next, I realized that I didn't know what a great flute tone sounded like, so I went to the library and checked out every recording they had of great flute players such as Renele Roy, Marcel Moyse, and Philippe Gaubert and listened to how they sounded. Then I tried to imitate it. And, the last thing I did was to try and communicate my feelings for someone through my music. I pretend to play to someone I care about and put that emotion into my playing. That way, music is my way of showing my feelings for that person."

Chrissy glanced at the ground as she spoke. Dale was wondering who she was playing for.

Mr. Jeffrey congratulated Chrissy on her hard work and preparation for her solo and noted that Chrissy had discovered what it is like to be a serious musician.

Mr. Jeffrey tapped his baton on the stand. "Let's go back and play the piece straight through. Remember to balance your sound to Chrissy's flute. I want you all to pretend you are playing to someone you care about." Bridget laughed nervously as she glanced at Dale.

At the end of the rehearsal, Mr. Jeffrey said, "After the concert in two weeks, you'll have your audition for me at the junior high. We've got a lot to get ready for. I want you to split your practice time between preparing for both performances. Now let's put things away and also remember, *Oskee Wow Wow.*"

The entire band erupted with *Oskee Wow Wow.* As the band members sauntered back to Mrs. Cooper's class, Dale caught up to Chrissy. He was about to ask her who she was playing to when P.J. ran up behind him and grabbed his music folder.

"Always be aware of your surroundings!" he said as he ran down the hall waving Dale's folder in the air.

After school, the gang met at the Jungle to do a little spring-cleaning after a long winter. They swept out the spiders and dirt from the fort, cut new branches to put in the camouflage netting and began collecting new dirt clods for the first game of Capture the Flag. They were so busy that the 5 o'clock whistle from the Conn factory startled them. It was time to go home for dinner.

P.J. and Dale parted ways at the fire station and each headed off toward home. Dale paused at the top of Simpson Hill and could see his home. Everything was eerily quiet. Grandpa wasn't on the porch waiting to give Scout a scratch and no one in the neighborhood was on the street. Even Scout perked up his ears and tilted his head from side-to-side. He trotted close to Dale's bike instead of racing toward the porch. Dale parked his bike at the back of the house and went in through the side door. The kitchen was empty, dinner was not cooking on the stove, and grandma didn't greet him.

"Stay close, Scout, something is wrong," he said as he walked into the kitchen.

He was about to call out when he heard the radio playing softly from the living room. As he entered the room, he saw his mom, grandma and grandpa listening to the radio intently.

Dale paused as the announcer said, "We now interrupt this scheduled program for an important announcement. Today at 4:35 p.m. President Franklin Delano Roosevelt died unexpectedly in Warm Springs, Georgia. The President was stricken by a cerebral hemorrhage dying at the age of sixty-three."

Chapter 9

UNEXPECTED FIRST

It had been a week since Dale heard the news on the radio. He felt an unusual sadness that the President, who had written him a letter, sent him dog tags, read his letter to the nation on the radio, and had sent orders to Fort Robinson to find Scout, had died. The entire nation during the last week had pulled together to support Vice President Truman who took over as President and vowed to carry on the late President's efforts to win the two world wars. In school, Principal Prenty had a moment of silence and asked all of the students to plant a victory garden in memory of the man who had led the nation during some of its most tumultuous times.

Grandfather helped Dale plant his victory garden by digging up the back yard by the alley where the plants would get good sunlight each day. Dale decided to grow pumpkins and watermelons and had bought the seeds himself.

But, today was very exciting for Dale and the gang because it was Friday and they were going to have the first race of the season after school. Everyone was ready to see who had gotten faster over the winter. Even today's band rehearsal seemed to drag on as each one tried to keep from thinking about the big race. Mr. Jeffrey was not very happy with the rehearsal that was only one week away from the concert. He had to admit that the warm sunny weather made him restless for the weekend, too. Once he realized the band was not as focused as usual, he switched up the rehearsal and played the more lively pieces.

Mr. Jeffrey decided to play a game he called *Quick Draw Scales* at the end of rehearsal. Two players at a time would come up to the front of the band and lay their instruments on the big table where music or handouts for the day were laid out. Each player would put his or her hand on their hips as if they were going to draw a pistol from a holster just like the cowboys did in the movies. Once the players were ready, he would shout out one of the scales the students were required to perform for the upcoming junior high audition. As soon as he called the scale, both players had to pick up their instruments and play the scale as fast as they could with no mistakes before the other player finished. The winner would then be challenged by a new player. After several rounds it came down to Dave on mallets against Bridget on her saxophone. Bridget had defeated everyone except Dave who asked that instead of putting his mallets on the table, he wanted to stick the mallets in his front pant pockets and draw them out like pistols in the westerns they watched.

Mr. Jeffrey thought about it for a moment. "OK, but you have to keep your hands by your sides until I finish calling out the scale."

Dave adjusted the mallets in his front pockets. "Fair enough," and he turned and faced the marimba with his hands by his sides.

Bridget set her saxophone on the table. "You're going down, Mr. Quick Draw," which made everyone laugh.

"OK, the scale I want you to play is...E-flat major," and before Bridget could get her saxophone to her mouth, Dave had drawn the mallets out of his pockets and was playing the scale."

"Winner," Mr. Jeffrey said as Dave finished the scale without any mistakes. He pretended to blow the smoke off of his mallets and put them back in his pockets.

The band was clapping and laughing when, Mr. Jeffrey said, "So you think you're the best in town? I challenge you." Mr. Jeffrey walked back to the percussion section and took a pair of mallets off the stand. "What do you say, Mr. Quick Draw?"

"You're on, Mr. Jeffrey, but someone else has to shout out the scale."

Dave searched through the sea of eager hands. "I want Victor to call the scale."

Mr. Jeffrey and Dave both adjusted their mallets in their pockets and stepped up to the marimba, their hands by their sides.

Victor thought for a second about what scale to call out. "The scale I want you to play is...C Major."

Like a flash Mr. Jeffrey drew the mallets out of his pockets while Dave froze. He proceeded to play the scale up and down with no mistakes.

"Winner," Victor said as Mr. Jeffrey finished the scale and pretended to blow the smoke off his mallets and placed them back in his pockets.

The band went wild laughing and clapping until Dave said, "I thought Victor would pick a really hard scale like A-flat. When he said C Major, the easiest one of all, I froze. OK, Mr. Jeffrey, you win...but I'll get my revenge next time."

"OK partner, now everyone clean up and get to class. Remember next week I want you focused on the concert. Agreed?"

"Agreed," the band responded and began putting the equipment away.

On the way back to class the band was still excited about the race and the weekend as they walked through the halls. As they entered Mrs. Cooper's class, she wasted no time getting the students' attention.

"I could hear you coming all the way down the hall! We have lots of work to do these last five weeks of school, and I don't want you to waste the educational time we have."

Bridget said, "Sorry, Mrs. Cooper. We're just excited about the race after school and the scale game that Dave thought he won. The best part was that Mr. Jeffrey beat him!"

"Thanks, Bridget. I can understand your excitement with all the warm weather and especially with your first race of the spring. I might have to come out myself and see who wins. I hear that some of you have been preparing all winter for this race."

"Who's been doing that?"

"It is not my place to say who. You'll just have to see."

The students looked at one another trying to figure out who she was talking about but whoever it was, she did not give it away. The rest of the afternoon, everyone stayed on task as the minutes ticked by. At five minutes to three Mrs. Cooper said, "When the bell rings you are excused. Enjoy your weekend and good luck at the race."

The bell rang and the students leapt up, and hurriedly packed up their instruments and books.

"Who do you think Mrs. Cooper was talking about?" Sandra said as the gang gathered in the hallway.

"I don't know, but she seems to have some inside information. Is it you, Dale?" Dave said.

"I have been doing PT with my Dad, but only for the last three weeks."

"I'll bet it's P.J.," Victor said.

P.J. was lagging behind the group. "You saw how slow I was racing Dale to school today. I can't believe you think I've been preparing for the race. And besides, I am the starter."

"Enough guessing! We'll have our answer when the race starts," Chrissy said as she began walking faster.

As they approached the track, they could see fresh white lines marking the lanes on top of the black cinders. There was a start line and a finish line. The lanes were also numbered from one to eight.

"Who put all the lines on so early in the spring? They usually don't do this until May for the Junior High District track meet," Tommy said as he set his rucksack and instrument on the bleachers and began stretching.

Tony, who was the judge for the race had ridden over from the junior high. "These lines will make it easier to see who wins."

The gang moved toward the starting line.

"Can I run in the first lane like the last race we had last fall?" Victor said.

"Sure, and don't forget to keep your head down and not look back," Bobby said.

As Victor moved to the first lane, Sandra said, "What do you have in your hand?" and she pointed at the little garden trowel that Victor had by his side.

"Oh, this is to dig my starting blocks. I heard that it helps you to push off the starting line and get a good start. I think I need all the help I can get."

"I'm just going to use my foot and dig a hole as usual," Dale said lining up in the second lane.

"Remember, no false starts or we'll have to have a restart," Tony said from the finish line.

Everyone got in the lanes. It was time to begin a new series of races and each one would try to defend his or her title or win for the first time.

P. J. was about to start the race when he saw Mr. Cabutti, their gym teacher, sitting on the school steps watching. "How come Mr. Cabutti is looking at us? You don't think he heard me imitating him and is mad or something."

"No, he probably heard about the race like Mrs. Cooper and just wants to see what happens. Come on, let's start this race." Victor said.

P.J. looked to the finish line. "Tony are you ready?" Tony waved that he was ready. P.J. turned to the racers. "Get down into your starting positions."

Each racer gradually got into position.

"On your mark...Get set...Go." and off they went. The sound of their shoes on the cinders and heavy breathing filled the air as the racers flew down the track. About half way through, Dale thought he heard someone yelling, but he quickly turned his attention back to his running. As the group neared the finish line, they raised their heads to hear Tony yell, "The winner is Victor!" Seconds before the next runner streaked across the finish line.

Silence fell over the gang as they caught their breath and slowly walked back to the finish line where Victor stood with a huge smile on his face.

"I can check that off my list," Victor said pretending to make a big check mark in the air.

"Tony, are you sure Victor won or are you kidding around like the last time?" Dale said.

"No, he won fair and square and in fact he led the entire race. He ran like a jack rabbit!"

P.J. added in his best Cabutti voice, "All your hard work paid off, Victor. Don't you think?"

Dale's eyes widened as Mr. Cabutti came up behind P.J.

Mr. Cabutti looked down at P.J. as the boy sputtered, "Sorry, sir!"

"That's OK. In fact, I'm honored that you'd use my voice as the starter. Sounds just like me, don't you think?"

P.J. nodded in relief.

"Either way, that was a great race. Congratulations to Victor for coming in first and Dale for being second."

"How'd you get so fast, Victor?" Sandra said still catching her breath.

"After the race where you let me win, I decided to ask Mr. Cabutti to help me learn how to run faster. I figured since he is the track coach at the junior high that he could help. I made him promise not to tell anyone. I thought Mrs. Cooper was going to give it away this morning, but luckily she didn't."

"Victor has been coming to the East Libertyville Junior High three times a week to run and do exercises and it's paid off. I hope next year you'll join the track team."

Then he turned to Dale. "The way you're filling out you

might make a great basketball player. In the winter I'm the junior and senior high boys basketball coach."

"Thanks, Mr. Cabutti," Dale said. "I like basketball and am always shooting hoops at home."

"I hope you liked the lines. I put them on so it would seem like a real race. I'll keep them fresh until graduation. Victor, you better watch out. Some of your friends are going to be ready for you next time."

"You sure can keep a secret, Victor. I'm impressed that you're the first to mark off one of the items on your list," Tommy said. "I thought that I'd be first since tomorrow we're going to the quarry. I'm going to swing on the rope and jump into the water."

"So I have two firsts. First to win a race and first to check off an item on a list!"

"Don't let it go to your head," Bridget said rubbing the top of his head. The rest of the gang followed her lead.

"Come on, let's get going," Charlie said rubbing his stomach. "I'm getting hungry, and remember, let's meet at ten o'clock sharp at Tommy's house to figure out how we're going to get the rope up in the tree."

"I can't wait," Chrissy said.

"Girls aren't allowed to come," Dave called as the boys made a run for their bikes.

Chapter 10

TOMMY

Saturday morning began with Dale running up Simpson Hill for the second time still thinking about Victor's miraculous victory. When he reached the top of the hill, he paused and thought that maybe he should attempt the hill a third time to build muscle for the next race. Scout barked twice and turned toward the house.

"Not yet Scout, one more time. If I'm going to beat Victor, I have to run more than usual." Scout turned only to see Dale running back down the hill. He barked again, but Dale continued down the hill. Scout relented and followed Dale back down.

After the third run up the hill, Dale was drenched in sweat. He sat on his back porch, breathing heavily. Scout's tongue was hanging out while he panted. Dale patted him on the head. "You look exhausted, Scout! Let's get some breakfast before we meet Tommy at 1000 hours." As Dale entered the kitchen door, he stopped suddenly. His father was sitting at the table with grandpa and grandma.

"When did you get back?" Dale said as he hugged his father.

"Right after you left for your morning PT. From all the sweat on your shirt and now mine, I'd say you really worked hard this morning. Go put a dry shirt on and wash the sweat off your face. When you're finished, you can have some breakfast and tell me about your week."

Dale took off up the stairs two at a time to change his shirt and was back down sliding into his usual chair at the table only to find a full cup of coffee with cream.

He leaned forward toward the cup. "I just like to smell the coffee," he said and inhaled deeply. Dad agreed.

"How come you're back so soon? I wasn't expecting you until tonight."

"I'm sure that you've heard that the attack on Okinawa has turned into a huge battle," and dad glanced down at his plate.

"I've been ordered back to the Pacific. The war in Europe is quickly drawing to a close. The Soviet Union began attacking Berlin from the east for the first time and the Germans have surrendered their Western front. It won't be long now until the United States achieves victory in Europe and that means an all-out effort to win the war in the Pacific. The military needs all experienced soldiers in the field now, so I must go back Sunday afternoon."

Dale sat quietly absorbing his father's words. Mother touched his hand.

"At least your father is here now. Let's enjoy the next two days. Why don't you tell him about your week?"

So Dale told his father all about school, band rehearsal and the race that Victor had won. Just then the large grandfather clock chimed 9:30, interrupting the conversation.

"I forgot what time it was! I've got to meet Tommy at ten." Dale excused himself from the table and put his dishes in the sink.

"What are you planning to do today?" Dad said.

"We're going to hang a rope swing from a tree that hangs over the quarry. It's one of the items on Tommy's list."

Mother furrowed her brow. "Wait a minute, young man! What tree and what rope swing?"

Before Dale could answer his dad spoke up. "Don't worry, mother. We've checked the tree and the depth of the water under the tree. We made sure there were no rocks or trees under the water and that it was deep enough. Dale knows better than to jump into water without knowing the depth or what might be under the surface."

"Be careful," she said glancing at Dad apprehensively.

Dale nodded and went to his room to change into his jeans and pack his swim suit. He returned to the kitchen to make some peanut butter sandwiches for lunch.

"I want to have your Dad's favorite dinner tonight, spaghetti, so don't be late," his mom said.

Scout bounded out the door after Dale, but his master said, "Sorry, today you stay here," and he hooked the dog's leash to the chain in the yard. "Enjoy your rest before tomorrow's PT," he added as he jumped on his bike.

The gang was waiting on the front porch looking at a piece of paper Tommy was holding.

"About time, Dale!" Tommy said as Dale slid to a stop.

"My dad came home early, and I lost track of time. Anyway, it's only 9:45. What's everyone looking at?"

"Tommy has drawn a diagram and has written out what needs to be done," Dave said. "But, I'm still confused how we're going to get the big tow rope to the Jungle? It sounds really heavy and long to me."

Tommy reassured them that he had it all figured out. "Let's meet Mr. Johansson down at his boat repair shop where the rope is. He's going to give us an old tow rope that was used to tie up barges. The rope has a loop at each end so we'll have an easier time tying the rope to the tree. We'll also have a foot hold when we swing out over the water. Dale, since you have the ruck sack, you can carry the climbing harness and spurs I got from my dad."

"Sure, but let me move my sandwiches so they don't get smashed."

"My dad taught me how to use the harness and spurs. We've been practicing on the trees out back so it should be no problem."

The boys mounted their bikes and started toward the hardware store. Victor said, "Let's not race! My legs are sore from the race yesterday."

"You're starting to whine like P.J.," said Tommy who was leading the pack.

"I don't whine, do I?" P.J. said as he raced ahead of Victor.

In front of the store, the boys skidded to a stop, each trying to beat each other's skid. Victor was the last to arrive

"I told you my legs are tired!"

"We still have to ride back to the Jungle with the rope. Mr. Johansson put it by the back door of the shop when I was here yesterday."

The boys ran around to the back of the building to find a rope coiled like a snake next to the back door. They stood in a circle and stared in admiration.

"How will we ever carry that?" Dale said lifting one end to test the weight.

"I've got it all figured out," Tommy said. "First we uncoil the rope and lay it across the parking lot. Next, we get our bikes and space ourselves equal distances apart along the rope. Then we pick it up with our left arm, and hang it on our left shoulder. Now, this is the hard part, so listen carefully. Once we have the rope balanced on our shoulders, we start riding together in one big line, holding the rope on our left shoulder while we steer our bikes with our right hand. If we all ride at the same speed we should be able to carry it to the Jungle. What d'ya think?"

"Easier said than done," Bobby said. "How'd you ever figure this out?"

"I got the idea watching a garter snake crawling on the ground by my house and thought we could do the same thing with the rope."

"Let's try it! It'll be fun to see if we can all move together," Bobby said as he picked up one end of the rope and began stretching it across the parking lot.

"Yah, you're right, this should be one memorable ride," Karl said helping to lay out the rope.

The rope stretched from one end of the parking lot to the other. Tommy called out the orders. "Get your bikes and space yourselves out equally. I'll take the front and Dale will take the back."

It took several minutes for the group to figure out the spacing. When Tommy was satisfied, he gave the final instructions. "Put the rope on your left shoulder. I'll count to three, and on three, we'll all push off and begin pedaling. Does everyone understand?"

"So if we all pedal at the same speed, you think we'll make it to the Jungle?" P.J. said.

Tommy checked to see that each boy had the rope on his left shoulder and would steer with the right hand.

"It's worth a try. Doing something for the first time is fun. And, this is definitely a first!" Dave said.

"I'll count to three before pushing off. Be sure to stay together."

Dale who was at the far end called, "Ready when you are!"

"Here we go! One ... two ... three," and all the boys pushed off, moving the rope forward.

P.J. and Victor were in the center and were slow to push off. The back of the rope went forward but the front of the rope did not move. The line of rope came to a halt with Victor crashing to the ground.

Victor struggled back up and brushed off his pants. "I didn't get a good push off that time. Let's try again."

After five attempts, the boys finally figured out how to move together.

"We did it!" Tommy said from the front as the line weaved out of the parking lot and onto Main Street.

Dale was the last one out of the parking lot. He yelled down the line, "You should see how funny this looks! We look like a snake." The undulating line of rope held by the boys moved down the street toward the Main Street businesses. People stopped and stared at the line of boys. Cars honked their horns and swerved so as not to hit the boys as they continued riding through the streets.

"Get out of the way!" Tommy commanded as he tried to steer the line of bikes. Dale heard a siren in the distance. He turned to see officer O'Malley's police car making its way through the crowded street.

"Tommy, stop! I think we're in trouble!"

The line of bikes wobbled to a stop just as officer O'Malley got out of his car. He walked down the line of bikes, shaking his head as he inspected the rope.

"What in tarnation are you boys doing?"

Tommy set his rope down and stepped forward. "If you have to arrest someone take me."

A crowd of people began to form around the boys and the policeman.

"Where are you going with this rope?" Officer O'Malley said.

Tommy stammered, "We're taking it to the Jungle to make a rope swing. This was the only way we could get it there."

The policeman scratched his head.

"This has to be a first for Libertyville. I can understand your plan, but look at the traffic jam!"

Someone from the crowd shouted, "Come on, O'Malley. Remember when you were young?" The crowd began to chant, "Let them go, let them go."

"OK ... OK ... let's all quiet down. I tell you what. If you boys promise not to carry any more rope through the streets, I'll let you go ... this time."

Tommy vowed for the group. "We promise!"

"Give me a minute to pull my squad car up to the front. I'll escort you to the Jungle."

The crowd parted as the officer turned on his siren, drove on the sidewalk to lead the boys down the street.

"Stay up with me!" and the policeman waved his hand out the window to signal the boys to follow.

"Let's get it right this time," Tommy said before counting to three and pushing off.

The boys held the rope, weaving down Main Street with officer O'Malley in front, the siren blaring. At the trail leading into the Jungle, the officer turned off his siren and got out of his squad car.

"Thanks, officer, for not arresting us," P.J. said.

"When you get the swing done, let me know. I'd like to try it. Now get this rope into the Jungle and off my streets before I change my mind."

Once the policeman drove away, Tommy said, "What a great police escort!"

"What do you mean? I almost threw up when I heard the siren," Bobby said.

Everyone laughed as they picked up the rope. "I think we'll walk it in from here," Tommy said.

After each boy had hidden his bike in the brush, they each went back to their spot on the rope and picked it up.

"This is a lot easier than riding," Dave said as the line of boys moved down the trail. Once they got to the oak tree, they set the rope down. The water in the quarry below shimmered in the sun. Dale brought out his stash of peanut butter sandwiches, one for each boy.

"Look what I took out of the cooler at the firehouse!" holding up a bottle of cola for all to see.

Karl licked his lips in disappointment. "You only brought one?"

P.J. triumphantly brought more bottles out of his ruck sack. "This is why I didn't want to fall down with that rope."

For the next half an hour, the boys lounged in the shade and planned how to get the rope up into the oak tree.

Tommy assigned each boy a task. First, he would climb the tree with his harness and climbing spikes. When he was high in the tree, he would have Karl, who had the best throwing arm of the bunch, heave a stick up to him which was tied with a piece of clothesline that Dale had borrowed from his grandmother. The big rope would be tied to the other end of the clothesline. The plan was for Tommy to catch the stick with the clothesline attached and pull up the big rope. He would then secure the rope on the limb that extended over the quarry. Finally, he would climb down while the other boys tied the clothesline to the bottom of the rope so that they could pull it back to the bank each time someone swung off the rope into the water.

"Does everybody understand what their job is?" Tommy said as he slid on his harness and climbing spikes.

"Are you sure you can climb all the way up there and then catch the stick without falling out of the tree?" Karl said as he shaded his eyes and looked up at the huge tree.

"My dad and I came here last week and practiced," and with that, he started climbing the tree while the others tied the clothesline to the stick.

Tommy climbed higher and higher until he stopped, dug his spikes into the trunk, and secured his harness.

"Now, throw that stick up here, and don't knock me out of the tree!"

Karl's first try didn't even get close. "Sorry, I didn't want to knock you out. I'll get it there this time."

The other boys shouted encouragement and suggestions as Karl stepped back to throw. This time the stick flew over Tommy's head and caught on the limb above him.

Tommy was able to stretch his arm and grab the stick with the clothesline. Hand over hand he tugged the line with the heavy rope attached up the tree. When he had the rope in his hand, he leaned out on the big limb and tied the rope to the branch before untying the clothesline.

He called down to the boys on the ground. "Be sure to tie the clothesline to the bottom of the big rope once I drop it. We don't want the big rope getting away."

Tommy dropped the rope to the ground. "Got it," P.J. said and Dale tied the clothesline to the bottom of the rope.

Once on the ground, Tommy looked back up. "That's really a long way up!"

"And a long way down!" Dave said testing the rope with his weight. "Feels good."

They changed into their swim suits and sat on the bank to decide who would go first.

"Since this is my idea, I'll go first," and Tommy took the big rope in his hands. "After I let go, Dale, pull the rope back in with the clothesline."

Tommy backed up as far as possible. "Here goes nothin'," and took off running toward the edge. At the last instant, he jumped into the air and swung out over the water. When the rope would go no further, he let go. The boys ran to the edge and watched him pull his legs together and fall toward the water below. As Tommy hit the water they cheered and waited for him to surface. After several seconds, Tommy popped up. "That was the best!"

"I'm next," Dale said grabbing the rope and handing the clothesline to Victor. "The holder of the clothesline is the next to jump." Dale pulled the rope duplicating Tommy's run and swung off the bank.

The boys took turns swinging into the water. On his first try, P.J. did a belly flop and emerged from the water with a bright red burn on his stomach. Dave followed with a cannon ball, and on the final jump, Karl executed a perfect back flip.

As Karl swam back to shore, the factory whistle blew.

The boys gathered their gear and secured the rope to the trunk of the oak. Tommy said, "Thanks for making the first item on my list a great time. I can't imagine how much fun we'll have with the rest of this Summer of Firsts."

Dale made sure he untied the clothesline that he had borrowed from his grandmother. He hoped she hadn't noticed it was missing.

"It's so hot that I'll just ride home in my swim suit and gym shoes," Dale said.

They jumped on their bikes and rode through the streets, dropping each boy off at his home. As they pulled up in front of P.J.'s house, Dale said, "You'd better put a shirt on. Your mom is going to be really mad when she sees your red stomach."

P.J. struggled into his shirt. "You have to admit it was the best belly flop ever!"

Dale continued up Simpson Hill. He could see mom, dad, and grandpa sitting on the front porch with Scout. Grandmother, however, was standing and intently looking his way with her hands on her hips.

He parked his bike in front, and as he walked up the porch steps, he noticed the basket full of wet clothes by Grandma's feet.

Before he could say anything, Grandma crossed her arms. "You have some explaining to do about why I have no clothesline. And, while you're at it, you can explain why our phone has been ringing off the hook with all of my friends telling me about you and your friends causing a mess downtown. What do you have to say for yourself?"

Scout slithered under the porch swing, his ears close to his head. Mom and dad stared at him, while grandpa turned to the side.

"Guilty on all counts! I did borrow the clothesline, but I did bring it back." Dale undid his ruck sack and handed the clothesline to Grandma. "And, about the mess downtown, it's true, but we didn't get arrested. In fact, we got a police escort with a siren. The crowd even clapped for us as we rode down the street." Dale scanned the faces for signs of possible support.

Grandpa leaned back, slapped his leg and began laughing, followed by dad and mom joining in. Grandpa admitted, "I was at the hardware store when I heard the siren and looked out the window to see seven boys holding a rope weaving in and out of traffic. I have to say it was the funniest thing I've ever seen!"

Grandma remained unconvinced. "Well, I wasn't there, and I don't think it's so funny."

"You should have seen the look on O'Malley's face when the crowd began chanting *Let them go, Let them go*!"

Grandma wiped her hands on her apron and shook her head. Dale looked her in the eye and took her hand. "I'm really sorry I disappointed you. I'll put the clothesline back, and I'll even hang up all the wet clothes," and he kissed her on the cheek and hurriedly left the porch, Scout tagging along behind.

"That will help get you back in my good graces," she said smiling at Dale who had picked up the laundry basket. "It must have been some sight to get Marge Larson to laugh as she told me the story over the phone. I don't think that old bitty has ever laughed." She turned and opened the door. "Let's have dinner. And, since your grandfather thinks your escapades are so funny, he can help you hang the clothes and do the dishes." Grandpa gave grandma an impish look, lumbered out of his chair, put his arm around her and cheerily, with a twinkle in his eyes said, "As you wish my dear."

Chapter 11

CHRISSY

As many had predicted, the war with Japan continued to build. The following week, Dale's father was called back overseas, a parting that was particularly painful for Dale. The two of them had shared so many special times since he and Scout had returned, and with the fighting in the Pacific accelerating, Dale couldn't bear to think that anything would happen to his dad.

On the European front, the nation had been shocked to hear about the troops liberating a concentration camp at Buchenwald, Germany. Dale's classmates discussed the news that the camp had been used to kill Jews. They didn't understand why a group of people would try to exterminate another group of people just because they were a different race or religion. Each day the news was filled with the horror that had taken place in Buchenwald. As more information about what really went on in the camp was revealed, America was even more determined to bring the war in Europe to an end.

After the weekend, the band members came back focused and ready to put the finishing touches on their concert. At the morning's final rehearsal, Mr. Jeffrey began each number, but he had them play only a short part so their lips would be fresh for the performance. Bobby, the first chair clarinetist, led the band into the auditorium and had them sit when he gave the signal. He also played a note for the band to tune. Between the second and third number, Bobby had to bring out a stand for Chrissy's solo and make sure that her music was placed properly on the stand. The practice wasn't so good. At first he set Chrissy's music on the stand upside down, and she had to frantically fix the pages. Another time the stand was too low, causing her to lean forward at an awkward angle. Mr. Jeffrey reminded Bobby in front of the band about being attentive to details since his mistake could affect the soloist's performance. Bobby slunk into his chair, determined not to make those mistakes at the concert.

At the end of rehearsal Mr. Jeffrey reminded the band about being on time and the proper clothes to wear for the concert.

The director closed his folder and spoke in a serious tone. "This first year of band has been wonderful, and I'm looking forward to the final Emerson School concert. I'm even more excited, however, about your upcoming auditions at the junior high. You're a special group, having been the first sixth graders in the history of this school to play in band," the director said. "We'll see you tonight!"

After the rehearsal, Bobby lingered until all the others had left. He stood next to the director who was trying to remove P.J.'s mouthpiece that had gotten stuck in the tuba's lead pipe. Tentatively, he said, "Are you sure you want me to be the one to lead the band and tune them and get Chrissy's music and stand ready?" he said sheepishly.

Mr. Jeffrey looked into Bobby's serious eyes. "Being the first chair clarinet is like being the first chair violin in an orchestra. In an orchestra, that violinist is called the concert master and in a band that is what you are. You are the musician's leader, and you must act like one. If I didn't have complete confidence in you, I wouldn't have you sitting first chair. You will do a good job, I know it."

Relieved Bobby said, "Thanks! I won't let you or the band down," and Bobby turned and ran happily down the aisle of the auditorium.

Back in the classroom, Bobby slid into his seat next to Chrissy. She leaned over and whispered warmly. "You'll do fine! If I'm not worried, then you shouldn't be either."

The rest of the day Mrs. Cooper had the students working independently on completing their book reports that were due next week Friday. Outwardly, the class seemed focused on their reports, but inwardly they were really thinking about the concert.

Dale looked around the room and could tell the song that was on each of his friend's mind. Dave's hands were tapping out his snare part to the opening march, *Amparito Roca*. Sandra was fingering the trumpet part of the second number *Concert Overture*. The room was alive with invisible music from the concert. Dale glanced at Chrissy who was sitting quietly with her eyes closed and her fingers moving in the precise patterns of her solo *Meditation from Thais*. He could see and hear her fingers tapping out all the phrases and runs of her solo. She was one with herself, and he marveled admiringly at her ability to concentrate.

Mrs. Cooper interrupted his thoughts. "It's almost time for class to end, and after seeing each of you practice your music for tonight during class, I can say it should be a great concert," to which the class smiled broadly. "Pack up your books and instruments and I'll see you tonight. Good luck, Chrissy, on your solo. As a former flute player myself, I'm looking forward to your song; it's one of my favorites." Chrissy felt deeply complimented because she liked and respected Mrs. Cooper and loved her class.

As the class filed out of the room, Dale watched Chrissy who was walking down the hallway with Bobby. The boy was shaking his head vigorously as if saying no. He could also see that she was very animated. It seemed as if she were trying to convince him of something, and he wasn't giving in. Dale decided to interrupt. "What are you two talking about? Seems like it's getting a little heated?"

Chrissy flashed a sharp look at Dale, signaling him to butt out. "No, we're not fighting. I'm just giving him a few pointers for tonight," she said poking him in the shoulder. Dale felt a little hurt and reluctantly fell behind them as they walked on chattering.

Before he could recover, she joined Bridget and Sandra who were impatiently waiting on the sidewalk.

Dale and Bobby joined the gang who were waiting at the bike rack. P.J. said, "That last look she gave you was really scary."

"Forget about it … it wasn't anything," Bobby said climbing on his bike.

"Leave him alone. He doesn't want to talk about it. How about I race you to the firehouse to get the dogs," Dale said as he ran to his bike, but P.J. had already pulled away so he could get a head start.

When Dale got home, his grandmother had a light dinner of cold roast beef sandwiches and chicken noodle soup set out.

"After the concert we'll have your favorite pie, pumpkin pie with whipped cream," and she was pleased with Dale's big smile of appreciation.

"I can't wait until the pumpkins and watermelons I planted in the victory garden with Grandpa are ready. Then we can make our own pumpkin pie."

"It'll take until August before they're ready. I'll teach you not only how to make the pies, but also the crust. A good crust is really important."

"I think after I eat, I'll water the garden before getting dressed, if that's OK."

"You'll have plenty of time to eat and water the garden before getting dressed. I set out your white shirt, red tie, and black pants. You might need to shine your black shoes one more time before the concert. Now eat your dinner and tell me about your day."

When Dale was finished, he found the hose and dragged it to the garden at the back of the yard. Scout took one look at the hose and ran back under the porch. Dale tried to coax him out, but Scout would have nothing to do with the hose and stayed under the porch. Grandpa had explained that pumpkins and watermelons needed three things: sandy soil; lots of sun; and lots of water. As Dale watered the plants, he could see the first blossoms beginning to open, as if popping in slow motion. Soon the bees would pollinate the blossoms, and then the pumpkins and watermelons would begin to appear. Just as he was finishing, he heard his mom's Jeep roar into the driveway.

"I can't wait until we can have some fresh watermelons," she said as she surveyed the rows of plants, putting her arm around Dale's shoulder. "Don't you think you should get ready for the concert?"

Dale set the hose down, gave his mom a nodding look and they walked back to the house to turn off the water. "Is grandpa coming tonight?"

"We're all coming, now scoot!"

When Dale got to his room, his concert clothes were draped over the chair and on his desk was a can of Shinola shoe polish and a rag. A note was propped up against his shoes.

I put a fresh coat of polish on your shoes this morning so you don't have to add anymore. Just give them a good buffing.

See you at the concert,
Grandpa

Grandpa was at the kitchen table finishing his dinner when Dale walked in. "Well, well!" he said in a bellowing voice. "Who is this young man?" He reached up to adjust Dale's tie. "You did a great job tying that tie. By the way, who taught you? Oh, that's right, I did!" he chuckled.

Grandma shooed the family out the door as the sun was slipping behind the trees. The spring evening was warm with a light breeze and helicopter seeds from the maple trees were circling downward in the air.

As the family pulled into the parking lot, a crowd was already streaming into the auditorium in hopes of getting good seats. P.J. met Dale at the door of the band room. "Did you see all the people coming?" he declared in a high-pitch voice. "I think I saw a bunch of band kids from East Libertyville Junior

High. I'm going to play great to show those older kids what a real tuba sounds like!" and he took his sleeve and buffed the bell of his tuba.

Dale set his case down and took out his cornet. The pearl valve covers glistened in the light. He leaned over to P.J. "Look, Chrissy is talking to Bobby again. What's that about?"

"I don't know, but from the look on her face, I'm staying out of it."

Chrissy turned and glanced at the other players before saying something to Bobby one last time and walking in a determined manner back to her seat. Bobby furrowed his brow and started warming up.

At exactly 6:15 p.m., Mr. Jeffrey stepped up to the podium, and everyone stopped playing. "Let's begin with some long tones." They continued by playing scales and started a few of the songs for the concert. Finally, Mr. Jeffrey tuned each section. At 6:50 p.m. Mr. Jeffrey closed his folder and said, "It's my pleasure to conduct you tonight. Remember what you've been taught and let's play great for Chrissy. She's worked hard and the highest honor you can pay a soloist is to play the accompaniment well so she can focus on her part." Dale was determined to do his very best.

The band began stomping their feet on the gym floor, but the director quickly stopped them. "Save your excitement for the auditorium. Bobby, they are all yours! Lead them in."

Bobby gave the band a firm thumb's up and proudly led them into the auditorium. As they filed out in their rows to the auditorium, the students were particularly quiet. When they walked on stage, Dale squinted into the lights and looked out into the crowded auditorium. He saw General Packston, the commander of the Air Force base, and his wife sitting next to Mr. Greenleaf, the owner of the Conn factory. Next to him was Joe Maddy the President of the National Music Camp at Interlochen and a tall gray-haired gentleman that Dale didn't recognize. Dale felt a bit light headed and had to take a deep breathe. His chair was on the right side of the podium, on the edge of the stage. As he stood waiting for the rest of the band to file in, he looked back at the audience and could see grandpa, grandma and mother smiling proudly from their seats to his left. Their being in the audience made Dale feel very special. Dale scanned the rows, but stopped when he noticed a group of kids all wearing the same type of jacket. There, right in the center of the auditorium, were students with matching black and yellow jackets emblazoned with the East Libertyville crest on the front.

P.J. bumped Dale's arm as he moved past him and whispered, "I told you those older kids would be here."

Dale didn't answer and adjusted his stand. Bobby looked back at the band, and once he was sure that they were ready, he sat down. The band followed. The musicians opened their folders and waited for Bobby to play Concert B-flat, the tuning note. Bobby played the note twice and then nodded to the band who would repeat the note. After each person made a small adjustment on his or her instruments, Bobby sat down.

The lights in the auditorium dimmed, and the stage lights brightened, illuminating the stage and making it almost impossible to see the audience. The audience applauded as Mr. Jeffrey walked onstage. When he reached the podium, he faced the audience and bowed slightly. Then he turned to the band, and with an encouraging smile, he stepped on the podium. Raising his baton, he gave the down beat for the march *Amparito Roca*. Then, Chrissy stood and walked off stage as planned to get ready for her solo while the band played *Concert Overture*. As the crowd applauded the second number, Bobby remained in his chair, looking down at his feet. Mr. Jeffrey motioned to Bobby to get Chrissy's music and stand, but again he didn't move. Mr. Jeffrey started to get the stand himself when the audience began clapping as Chrissy walked out on stage. Mr. Jeffrey gestured for her to wait until her stand was ready, but she lightly raised her hand, signaling him to stop. She walked to her place next to the podium. Right before turning to bow to the audience, she looked over at Bobby and Mr. Jeffrey and smiled. Dale couldn't believe it. *Was Chrissy going to play without music? How could she be smiling?* Bridget glanced quickly at Sandra and raised her eyebrows. Mr. Jeffrey nodded to Chrissy who returned the nod that she was ready. Mr. Jeffrey turned to the band, showing no emotion on his face. He raised his baton, gave the downbeat and Chrissy began to play.

The first note was full and round, leading into a triplet that pushed to a high D that was strong and clear. The beginning accompaniment was only woodwinds, so Dale leaned back and listened intently as she played. As Chrissy continued to play, her eyes closed in concentration, her flute moving up and down to the rhythm of the music, she gained confidence. When the brass joined in, the piece built toward an emotional climax. Gradually, the music got softer as the instruments dropped out of the accompaniment. Finally, the original melody returned. Chrissy took the last breath and pushed the eighth-note triplets for one last emotional phrase, ending on a low D before fading away.

After the piece had ended, she remained frozen, holding the flute to her lips and savoring the silence of the huge auditorium. When she brought her instrument down, the crowd erupted into thunderous applause. Dale could see the junior high students talking to one another, pointing at the stage.

From the front row, the gray-haired man jumped to

his feet, clapping and shouting "Bravo, Bravo!" The band stomped their feet loudly on the stage. Mr. Jeffrey stepped off the podium and backed away so that Chrissy could receive the audience's appreciation. He then came forward, shook her hand and whispered to her which made her smile. Chrissy bowed again, and then walked over to Bobby and shook his hand before pointing at the band and mouthing the words "Thank you!" As Chrissy went back to her seat in the band, Mr. Jeffrey held up his hand for the crowd to be quiet.

"Before we continue with the concert, I'd like to recognize the arranger of that composition who is here with us tonight. Dr. A.A Harding, the Director of the University of Illinois Concert Band, will you please stand." Slowly, Dr. Harding stood and waved at the audience. He then turned, pointed at Chrissy and bowed to her. Over the applause P.J. yelled, "Oskee Wow Wow!" which caused the crowd to laugh. Mr. Jeffrey motioned for the band to settle down, and the concert continued. Finally, it was time for Dale's favorite piece, a *Salute to the Armed Forces*. Mr. Jeffrey went to the microphone one last time.

"This has been a great year beginning with Dale and P.J. saving the Conn factory and Mr. Greenleaf donating the instruments you see on stage tonight. But, more important, I want to thank all of you for supporting a new generation of musicians. Over the past several years, America has been fighting in two world wars. I wanted to arrange a piece for the men, women, and families who have fought and supported the war effort. Our final number will be a salute to the armed forces. When you hear the song that represents the branch of the military that you either are serving in, have served in, or have family members serving in, please stand and be recognized."

Mr. Jeffrey moved to the podium and gave the down beat. Dave played a crisp buzz roll on the snare drum, followed by a traditional roll off.

The first branch of the military theme song played was the Marine's *From the Halls of Montezuma* followed by the Army's *U.S. Field Artillery Song* that was penned by John Philip Sousa and based on the song *As the Caissons Go Rolling Along*. The Coast Guard melody was next with *Semper Paratus* which means "Always Ready" followed by the Navy's *Anchors Away*. The medley ended with the Air Force's *Up in the Air*. During the final song, the crowd clapped in time with the band. After the final note, the crowd, applauding, jumped to their feet.

Mr. Jeffrey invited the audience to join the band for punch and cookies in the lobby after the concert. The crowd applauded again and Bobby led the band out in orderly rows back to the gym.

By the time Dale got to the gym, he found Chrissy jumping up and down and hugging Bobby saying, "Thanks so much for not telling anyone, especially Mr. Jeffrey, about not wanting any music or a stand brought out." Before Bobby could answer, a loud voice cut in. "I have to shake the hand of the soloist who made my arrangement proud." Chrissy blushed, as Dr. Harding grasped her hand and the students gathered around in awe.

"You were magnificent and to play from memory at your young age, well that's remarkable. I hope that after high school you'll consider playing in the University of Illinois Band, the best band in the land."

Mr. Jeffrey stepped in to join them. "She's not only remarkable, but shocking. I couldn't figure out why Bobby wasn't moving your stand or why you were coming out before the stand was ready. You almost gave me a heart attack! Come on Dr. Harding, I'll take you out front to meet some of the parents."

"Wait, wait." Dr. Harding said, "I have one more thing to say and that is OSKEE WOW WOW."

The band shouted back in unison, "OSKEE WOW WOW!" and they swarmed Chrissy to congratulate her.

Dale had been standing by his case until the crowd around Chrissy had left and she had put her flute away. "I wanted to wait until you were alone to give you these," he said handing her some lilacs tied together with a satin ribbon. "My grandma said I could cut these for you, so I hope you like them. You played so well, I don't know what else to say."

Chrissy held the flowers up to her nose, taking a deep breath of the fragrant blooms. She looked directly into his brown eyes. "You don't have to say anything, Dale. The flowers say it all."

Before he could answer, P.J. burst through the door of the gym. "Come on you're missing all the food."

Dale and Chrissy both laughed and together slowly moved toward the gym exit. She said, "P.J. is always interrupting us, but either way, the first item on my list is checked off!"

Chapter 12

TENSION BUILDS

Dale had never thought of his life in days, but each day since the concert had been memorable. On Friday after the concert, Chrissy won her first race of the year, and Mr. Jeffrey announced he would be starting a jazz band that would meet twice a week during school. On Saturday, the boys spent the day playing army and using Tommy's new rope swing to jump off into the quarry's cool water.

When Dale got home that night, he listened to the radio with his family. The announcer told about how the Italian dictator Mussolini was captured and hanged by the citizens of Italy after years of being tortured under his power. On Sunday night, as Dale lay on the living room carpet, he heard how the Seventh Army liberated another concentration camp in Germany, Dachau. The booming voice on the radio announced that this was yet another atrocity committed by Adolf Hitler's regime. Then on Monday, April 30, they listened to reports that Hitler had committed suicide to avoid being captured by the Russian and Allied forces that were closing in. The end of the war in Europe seemed to be quickly approaching. Two days later on May 2nd Germany and Italy surrendered to the Allied forces. People around the world listened and prayed for an end to the war and the safe return of their loved ones.

As Dale finished his Saturday morning PT with Scout, his thoughts focused on his audition today at East Libertyville Junior High. He had been practicing his audition music that consisted of playing several major and minor scales and a two-octave chromatic, and several etudes from the Arban's book. The final requirement was to sight-read. Sight-reading was difficult because a musician had to play a piece of music seen for the first time. Everyone would be given a new piece of music, have a minute to look at it and practice, and finally play through it with no stops. Mr. Jeffrey explained that he would give each student a series of progressively harder pieces to sight-read until the person could go no farther. Mr. Jeffrey had taught them a four-step process for sight-reading, which Dale reviewed in his head as he finished his sit-ups. With each sit-up, he would recite one of the steps: "Key, time, how loud, how fast. Key, time, how loud, how fast. Key, time, how loud, how fast." As Dale finished his last sit-up, he heard his mother.

"Dale, what are you saying?"

"They're the steps to reading a new piece of music. I want to get them in my head before the audition today."

"I have to get to the base, and you'd better eat breakfast before your audition," Mother said as she jumped in the Jeep and peeled out of the driveway.

"I could hear you reciting something in the garage. What did you call it?" Grandmother asked as Dale entered the kitchen. Grandma set a big plate of scrambled eggs and sausage in front of Dale.

"The four steps to sight-reading."

"That's right. Are you looking forward to playing in the band next year?"

"Yes and no. I'm looking forward to playing, but I'm a little nervous about playing with older students. Plus, some of the junior high band kids came to our last concert and I swear, one of them pointed at me. He was a dark-haired kid."

"I wouldn't worry. Anyway, why would a kid point at you?"

"You're probably right, but I swear he was. Either way, today will be a new adventure. I guess we have to grow up sometime. At least that's what grandpa says."

"I'm not sure grandpa has grown up yet. He still likes to do new things just like he did when he was your age." As she turned to flip more sausages that were frying in the pan, grandpa walked in the room.

"You're right. I haven't grown up. I guess I'm just a kid at heart."

"Good, we can be kids together," Dale said. "Oh, and speaking of learning something new, you should hear all the jazz we learned to play this week."

"I love jazz and swing dancing," grandpa said taking grandmother by the waist and spinning her around.

"Mercy, do behave! Now sit down and I'll get you some breakfast," grandma said, blushing as she moved to the stove.

Dale laughed as he put his plate in the sink and headed upstairs to get ready for the audition.

When Dale returned, grandpa had already left for work. "I missed saying goodbye to grandpa," Dale said as he packed his instrument and books in his ruck sack.

"He has to take a freight train to Marble Head with a load of soy beans, but he'll be back for dinner. He said you both could listen to the radio about the war tonight when he gets home."

"After the audition, the gang is going to the Jungle to swim and use Tommy's new rope swing. I'll come home when I hear the five o'clock whistle. See ya later," Dale said as he ran out the back door and whistled for Scout. "Come on, boy! Let's go get P.J. and Smokey."

Scout barked twice and took off for the fire station with Dale in hot pursuit. When they arrived, P.J. and Smokey were waiting patiently at the curb.

"About time! Let's hurry and get these dogs tied up so we can get to the junior high," P.J. said as he went to the back of the station to tie up the dogs.

"I'm not running late, you're just in a hurry," Dale said as he finished tying Scout to the rope.

"Remember, to be on time is to be late and to be early is to be on time."

"You're right. Let's pick up the gang on the way."

Dale helped P.J. get the big duffle bag with the tuba on his back being careful not to stand too close. They rode their bikes to the junior high that was about two miles away, and luckily for P.J., mostly downhill. Every few blocks, one of the gang would be waiting for them on the corner. By the time they got to the junior high, Karl, Victor, Bobby, Dave, and Tommy had joined the group. They were quite a sight, riding down the street with instruments hanging from one hand or strapped on their backs.

"Would you look at how big this school is?" Tommy said as they pulled up to the bike rack.

"I'll bet you could put five Emerson Schools in this place. I hope I don't get lost," Bobby said as he slid to a stop next to Dale.

"We might have to ask someone where the band room is," Dale said as he left the gang at the bike rack and started walking up toward the steps where some boys were sitting.

Dale counted eight boys. As he approached, one of the boys turned around and faced him. Dale stopped dead in his tracks when he recognized the boy he had seen at the concert, the one who had pointed at him.

"Can you tell me where the band room is? We're here for the auditions with Mr. Jeffrey. I'm Dale Kingston," Dale said as he reached the bottom of the steps.

The dark-haired boy stepped forward, "Yah, we know who you are. We've been waiting for you."

"You have?" Dale said taking a step back as the dark-haired boy moved down the steps. The other boys followed.

Dale turned to see where his friends were, hoping they would be behind him, but they were still at the bike rack.

"I don't think your friends can help you now," the dark-haired boy said. "We know who you are. You're that hot-shot cornet player from Emerson School we've been hearing about for the last several months. And, aren't you the 'hero' who saved the town with your bugle and got to play with the Andrews Sisters? If so, then that would make you Dale Kingston, wouldn't it?" The dark-haired boy took a few more menacing steps toward Dale.

Dale didn't answer as his heart pounded in his chest.

"What's the matter big shot? Cat got your tongue? I'm Jim Petris, and don't think you're coming to my school and taking over. You're on my turf, and don't you forget it."

Dale could feel his anger building, but before he could answer, P.J. pushed past Dale, running up the steps. His tuba duffle bag swaying on his shoulders, knocked against Jim, causing him to lose his balance momentarily.

"Watch out, tuba boy," the dark-haired boy said in a sinister manner. P.J. stopped, and as he swung around to see who said something, he knocked another boy off the step. Each time he turned to see who he had hit, he bumped into another boy, until they had moved several steps away from Dale. Victor, Dave, Tommy, Bobby and Karl came up behind Dale to see what was going on.

Victor stepped forward and stood next to Dale. "Did you find out where the band room is?" Then looking at the dark-haired boy and then back at Dale, he said, "Is there a problem? Who's your new friend?"

"He's not a friend," Dale answered angrily, "And, he hasn't told me where the band room is yet," Dale said staring straight into Jim's eyes.

"The band room is up the stairs to the right," Jim said, and he leaned toward Dale and slapped him on the back. "And don't forget what I said, hot shot!"

P.J. looked confused. "Is he talking to me or you? Either way, I don't like him"

Dale continued up the steps surrounded by his friends. "Let's forget those guys and play our audition."

The transition from the bright morning sun to the dark foyer of the junior high took a moment. When their eyes had adjusted to the dark, another group of older students were waiting for them. "Don't tell me, more trouble," Tommy said swallowing hard.

A tall boy wearing the yellow and black colors of East Libertyville came forward. "Welcome to ELJH. You must be from Emerson School. I'm Joey, and we're ninth graders in the band who are helping Mr. Jeffrey with the auditions." He stepped forward to shake their hands. "You can call me Red. That's what everyone calls me."

"I like your nickname," P. J. said shaking Red's hand. "My name is Charlie Walsh and I play the tuba. My friends call me P.J."

"Glad to meet you, P.J." Then he turned to Dale. "I've heard about you. Aren't you Dale Kingston? Come on, we'll show you where to warm-up."

Red and the other ninth grade band members lead the boys down the marble hallway. "This junior high may seem scary," Red said, seeming to understand their apprehension, "but you'll find that band is like a team sport ... we support each other." Red held the door to the warm-up room, and the boys entered. Dale paused and looked back down the empty hallway, thinking that both the tough boy on the steps and Red had known who he was. "I sure hope I can step up to everyone's expectations about my playing."

Chapter 13

THE AUDITION

Dale took one last look down the dark hallway before entering the warm-up room. The boys unpacked their instruments and sat in chairs while they waited their turn.

Every fifteen minutes or so, one of the ninth graders would escort someone to the band room to play for Mr. Jeffrey until the only one left in the room was Dale. He fidgeted with his valves, unable to get the confrontation with Jim out of his mind until Red returned. "You're next. Just remember, at one time, I was just as young and nervous as you." Dale looked up at the tall boy who seemed so self-assured. "You'll be fine. Now go and show Mr. Jeffrey your stuff. Follow me."

Dale followed Red down the hall to the band room. *Red was right,* he thought. He had practiced and prepared the best he could, so being nervous would serve no purpose. He took a deep breath as Red held the door to the band room open.

"Good luck!" and as the door closed, Dale watched through the door's window as Red turned and went back down the hallway.

Dale's eyes swept the band room. Large silver trophies lined the walls and there were pictures of past bands, the students wearing matching uniforms, sitting in neat rows. Row after row of chairs and stands sat ready for rehearsal. Bass drums, snare drums, and marimbas lined the back wall and wire cages full of instruments were on either side of the room.

"What do you think of your new rehearsal room?" Mr. Jeffrey said from his chair in the front row. "Big, isn't it?" He pointed to a chair. "Have a seat. You face the door, and I'll sit here in front and listen."

"This place is huge," Dale said and he sat in the chair.

"In another year, this room will seem small. Why don't you play a few long tones and get a feel for what you sound like. Victor already stopped in the middle of his audition like he did at the Easter service rehearsal and commented about how great he sounded in here."

Dale played his major, minor, and chromatic scales from memory. Mr. Jeffrey then asked him to play sections of the Arban's etudes. It was now time for the sight-reading.

"Open the binder in front of you. You'll be given one minute to look at the first page of sight-reading examples. You can play, sing, clap, count out loud, or do anything you want during that minute. Once the minute is up, you'll play the piece straight through. If you play well, you'll turn the page and play the second example. We'll continue until you're no longer able to play them accurately. Do you understand?"

Dale nodded.

"OK, open the binder and you have one minute."

Dale opened the binder and immediately thought about the four steps of sight-reading.

*First, the KEY is Bb, so I must play two flats, Bb and Eb. Second, the TIME is 4/4, so there are four beats in a measure and the quarter note gets one beat. Third, is HOW LOUD, and I have **mp** or moderately soft followed by a **crescendo sign** which means to get louder to **f** or a full sound. Then I have to **decrescendo** or get softer to an **mf** a moderately full sound. I'll stay at that volume until the **crescendo** on the second line to a **forte** where I'll play loud until the end. The fourth step is HOW FAST and **Andante** means at a walking tempo between 76 and 108 beats a minute.*

After the four steps, Dale clapped and counted the rhythms adding in the dynamics and played the scale that matched the key. Mr. Jeffrey called time and asked Dale to play.

The four-step process worked, and Dale was able to play four pages of sight-reading with no mistakes.

"Dale, this will be your last page of sight-reading. You can turn the page and begin your minute now."

Just as the time began, Dale looked up at the band room door. Through the glass, he saw Jim staring at him. Dale looked back into his dark eyes until Mr. Jeffrey interrupted. Just as the director turned, the dark hair boy ducked down. "I don't see anything out there."

Dale looked back at the door one last time. "Sorry, I just got distracted. I'm ready now."

"Your minute starts now." Dale kept glancing back at the door, unable to think about the four steps. Then Mr. Jeffrey called time and asked him to play straight through.

Dale put the cornet to his lips and bobbled the first note. He missed the next rhythm and ended up playing the piece too soft and slow. He also missed several sharps. Mr. Jeffrey sat quietly and jotted down a few comments in his notebook.

"Sorry ... I just got nervous," Dale said gazing at the window where the boy had been. "It won't happen again."

"I hope not. I know you can play better than that, so I'll assign you to a chair in the band for the fall."

Dale shook Mr. Jeffrey's hand and walked down the long, dark hallway to the warm-up room, disappointed that he had not played his best. As he turned the corner to the entrance of the building, Jim stepped out from the shadows of the foyer.

"Sounds like the hot shot messed up. Too bad!" and he put his hands up as if he were playing cornet, mocking Dale. "In the fall, I'm going to show you what real playing is like."

Before Dale could answer, Jim turned and walked out the entrance and he joined his friends who were laughing.

Dale's head was spinning when he heard footsteps coming up behind him. He spun around, only to see Chrissy, Bridget, and Sandra coming down the hall with Red on their way to the warm-up room.

"How'd it go?" Bridget said lightly as they walked by.

"Good luck on your auditions," he said. The girls were so interested in talking to Red that they didn't notice that Dale hadn't answered the question.

Dale stepped out the door and into the warm late morning sun. He looked in the direction that Jim and his friends had gone, but he didn't see anyone.

"What are you looking for? We're over here!" Tommy said from the bike rack. "Let's go to P.J.'s for lunch and then to the rope swing. I need to let off some steam. That was a tough audition."

Dale took a big deep breath. "Let's race to the fire house and get the dogs." He ran to his bike as his friends took off.

They spent the afternoon swimming and jumping from the rope swing. Before they rode home, they basked like lizards in the sun on the warm granite rocks.

"That sure was a tough kid," Tommy said. "What do you think his problem is?"

Victor turned over and put his hands behind his head. "I'll bet he's not so tough without his friends."

"I'm not sure what to think yet, but I don't trust him," Dale said.

"Don't worry about him, Dale. You're the best player, and you've got us. We always protect our own," Karl said.

Dave changed the subject. "Did you get a look at those ninth grade girls? I think they were giving me the eye."

"So you think those girls would be interested in YOU? Come on, Don Juan, I just heard the five o'clock whistle blow," Dale said.

Mother, grandpa, and grandma were sitting on the porch when Dale and Scout returned. During the ride home, he had decided not to tell them about the incident with the tough boy. Instead, he would just talk about the audition and the day at the Jungle.

"You look worn out," Mother began. "You must have had an exciting day."

Before Dale could answer, the fur on Scout's back raised, and he emitted a low growl. Dale turned to see Jim riding slowly down the street, looking directly at him. Dale took a hold of Scout's collar. "Lay down!" he said as his eyes followed Jim who turned to ride down Simpson Hill and out of sight.

As Dale sat back down, he thought to himself, *what's he doing on my block?*

Chapter 14

ONE DOWN, ONE TO GO

Dale had not slept well during the past week. Last Saturday seemed like a distant memory with all of the excitement and the news about a possible end to the war in Europe. As the family sat around the radio listening to the regularly scheduled jazz program, it was interrupted by special bulletins about the events unfolding in Europe. News of the battle for Berlin and the possible unconditional surrender of Germany filled the airways. At the end of the school day, Principal Prenty announced that Tuesday had been declared a holiday and that no school would be held. He explained that German General Alfred Jodl had signed an unconditional surrender in Reims, France. The agreement would be confirmed at nine o'clock on Tuesday morning when President Truman would speak to the country.

Mrs. Cooper's classroom burst into applause in hopes that the war with Europe would come to an end.

"Quiet down," Mrs. Cooper said in her loud voice. "We still have thirty minutes left in the school day." Tommy raised his hand.

"Where is Reims, France, and what does unconditional surrender mean?"

As Mrs. Cooper pulled down a giant map of Europe and North Africa from the tubes that hung above the blackboard, she explained that unconditional meant without conditions or not limited by a condition or circumstances. Germany had to totally surrender.

"Now, let's refresh our memories about where France is." Mrs. Cooper said as she picked up the wooden pointer. "Reims is in the northeastern part of France. Now look farther to the northeast, and you will see Germany and the city of Berlin. Can anyone tell me how we would figure out the distance from Reims to Berlin?"

Waving hands went up around the room to get Mrs. Cooper's attention. "Remember waving your hand back and forth will not get you called upon," Mrs. Cooper said as she scanned the room and called on Dave.

"May I come up and show you?" Mrs. Cooper nodded.

"Can I borrow your pointer?" Dave said moving to the front of the room.

"No, but you may use the pointer."

"Sorry, may I use your pointer?"

"Do be careful with this."

"If you look on the bottom right-hand corner you will see something that looks like a ruler. This is called a scale and all maps have them. It tells you that every inch of the map represents so many miles. On this map, one inch equals 100 miles. If I take this yardstick and put one end on the city of Reims and the other on the city of Berlin, and then I count the inches on the ruler between the two, I'll get the number of miles."

Dave did a little calculating. "It looks like four inches and," he looked carefully at the yardstick, counting the tick marks, "eleven-sixteenths."

"Very good! Now, I'd like everyone to take out some paper and figure out the mileage. Raise your hand when you have the answer."

Dave went back to his desk and began working on the problem with the rest of the class.

Karl raised his hand first, and Mrs. Cooper had him explain the problem on the board. Karl grabbed a piece of chalk and proceeded to explain each step in detail.

"I think you're ready to graduate to seventh grade! Now remember to listen to the radio tomorrow, and enjoy your holiday from school!"

The next morning, as Dale did his final sit-up for PT, he could smell bacon cooking in the kitchen. He grabbed his towel to wipe off the sweat and then burst into the kitchen.

"I knew the smell of bacon would get you in here!" grandma said cheerily. "I'll bet you could hear my stomach growling all the way from the garage," Dale said taking a seat.

"When aren't growing boys hungry?" Dale's mom said sitting down at the table.

Grandpa set the paper down. "From the news, today should be a day to remember," and he glanced at Dale. "And I don't mean just because there is no school."

"We are going to the fire house and I told P.J. that we were going to listen to the President speak this morning. What do you think he will say?"

"I don't know, but if the war in Europe has really ended, then we can turn our efforts toward the Pacific and hopefully get your dad home," mom said.

"I sure miss him," Dale said taking a swig of his fresh coffee.

"We all do," grandma said. "But, even if the war ends today, you'd better water that victory garden before you leave. It's looking pretty dry out there."

After breakfast, Dale watered the garden. Scout came out from under the porch to join him. He could see the plants starting to spread across the ground. "Looks good, doesn't it Scout?" But, before Dale could finish, Scout's fur on his back began to stand up and he lifted his lip in a growl. Dale bent down to calm the dog. He shaded his eyes and surveyed the backyard by the alley, but he didn't see anything.

Dale stood up and said, "Let's go meet the gang." He whistled to get the dog's attention, and then he ran to his bike and started toward the firehouse. Scout took one last look toward the alley before chasing after his master.

When Dale got to the firehouse, Mr. Walsh was just tuning in the radio. The front doors to the station were open, and Dale parked next to the other bikes and went inside with Scout. "Where is everyone?"

"Up here," Tommy said from the back of one of the trucks. "We thought we would sit up here and listen."

Scout joined Smokey in the back of the truck, and Dale picked a spot next to the hoses that were curled in neat piles.

P.J. came sliding down the brass fire pole. "Save me a seat, will yah?" he said as he landed on the floor.

Then the radio announcer said, "We interrupt this regularly scheduled program to bring you a message from the President of the United States."

Mr. Walsh hushed the group. The station was so quiet that Dale could hear Scout panting after the morning run to the firehouse.

President Truman began:

"This is a solemn but a glorious hour. I only wish that Franklin D. Roosevelt had lived to witness this day. General Eisenhower informs me that the forces of Germany have surrendered to the United Nations. The flags of freedom fly over all Europe. For this victory, we join in offering our thanks to the providence that has guided and sustained us through the dark days of adversity. Our rejoicing is sobered and subdued by a supreme consciousness of the terrible price we have paid to rid the world of Hitler and his evil band. Let us not forget, my fellow Americans, the sorrow and the heartache that today abide in the homes of so many of our neighbors—neighbors whose most priceless possession has been rendered as a sacrifice to redeem our liberty. We can repay the debt which we owe to our God, to our dead and to our children only by work—by ceaseless devotion to the responsibilities which lie ahead of us. If I could give you a single watchword for the coming months, that word is—work, work, and more work. We must work to finish the war. Our victory is but half won. The West is free, but the East is still in bondage to the treacherous tyranny of the Japanese. When the last Japanese division has surrendered unconditionally, then and only then will our fighting job be done."

As the President finished his speech, Dale's thoughts turned to his father who was in the Pacific, some eight thousand miles away. *Maybe his dad was listening to the same speech.*

No one spoke for a few minutes. The silence was interrupted by the sound of church bells, and the Conn factory whistle was blaring. Mr. Walsh jumped up and switched on the firehouse alarm bell. Libertyville was celebrating the end of the war in Europe. Scout and Smokey began barking, and Karl put his hands over his ears. Just then, the boys could feel the engine of the fire truck rumble to a start. Mr. Walsh stuck his head out the front window. "Let's drive around and celebrate with the town!"

The boys could not believe they were going to ride in the back of the fire truck with the sirens on. They held on as the truck drove out of the station, heading toward the town square. Business men and women, housewives, and children were out on the sidewalks celebrating the end of the war. But, just as quickly as the celebration had started, the crowd began to take on a more somber tone. Mr. Walsh turned off the siren and went back to the firehouse. P.J. said to his dad, "Why did all the people stop celebrating?"

"I think the people of Libertyville and the country realize that hard times and sacrifice are not over. We may have won the war in Europe, but we're still at war with Japan."

Dale's thoughts returned to his dad for a moment as he realized that Mr. Walsh was right ... there was still another war to win.

The boys climbed down from the back of the truck. Tommy broke the silence.

"Since this is a day off from school, we should have some fun."

Bobby agreed. "The sun is really warming things up. Let's grab some sandwiches and go to the Jungle," he said jumping on his bike to get a head start.

The boys eagerly chased after Bobby, but Dale was the last to leave. *One war down and one to go before you come home* he thought sadly and longingly, as his father's face flashed before his eyes.

Chapter 15

DIXIELAND JAZZ

It had been two weeks since the victory in Europe, or VE Day, when President Truman announced that Germany had surrendered. For the sixth graders at Emerson School, this week would be the last week of class before graduating and moving to the seventh grade. After the band's last concert, Mr. Jeffrey started having jazz band rehearsals twice a week and band only once a week. Dale found jazz challenging but also fun.

Dale, Bobby, Dave, Karl, P.J. Chrissy, and Bridget had even convinced Mr. Jeffrey to help them form a Dixieland jazz ensemble. They wanted to meet during the summer, and this smaller group would allow them to continue playing and learning jazz. Mr. Jeffrey thought that, with some hard work, they might be good enough to perform at the 4th of July celebration on the square.

P.J. and Dale parked their bikes. "Doesn't it feel strange to think we have four and a half days left of grade school and Mrs. Cooper?" Dale said.

"A little bit I guess, but I haven't thought about it too much, since I've been learning to play the string bass for jazz band. It's not too bad because both tuba and the string bass parts are in the same clef," P.J. said. "Race ya to the auditorium," and he sped off toward the school with Dale in hot pursuit.

As they entered the auditorium, Mr. Jeffrey, Bobby, and Dave were putting Dave's drum set together on stage.

"Do you want me to get some stands?" Dale said, setting his cornet case down.

"We won't need them. Why don't you help Bridget and Chrissy move the piano on stage. Then get your instruments out and warm up," Mr. Jeffrey said tightening the last bolt on the drum set.

Once everyone had warmed up, Mr. Jeffrey joined them with his cornet.

Chrissy's eyes widened as she scooted her piano bench toward the keys. "Are you going to play with us?"

"I'm going to demonstrate, because it's easier if you hear how jazz sounds. Today, we'll learn the basics of jazz, which includes chords and the blues progression. Tomorrow we'll read the two songs I've selected."

"Wait a minute! You mean we don't get any music today?" Karl said.

"Not today. The kind of music we're going to learn was

first learned by rote or playing by ear. Many early Dixieland musicians couldn't read music, so they learned to play a song by listening to it. They'd play the song over and over again until they could play it from memory. I'll go slowly at first so you can catch on. Before we start, let's talk about the history of Dixieland. If you don't know the history, you can't really fully appreciate this music."

Mr. Jeffrey explained that Dixieland developed over a long period of time. It was a blend of many different styles of music, including opera, military marching band, folk music, the blues, church, ragtime, and traditional African drumming. The instruments typically used were the cornet, trombone, clarinet, drums, tuba or string bass, and sometimes saxophone.

"Let's learn our first series of chords or a blues progression. Chrissy, I know your piano teacher taught you these chords, so I'll have you play the three chords that'll be in our first piece." Mr. Jeffrey went to the board and wrote three chords. "You'll notice that these chords are always notated with Roman numerals instead of numbers. First please play a (I) chord in B♭."

Chrissy played the chord and said, "Isn't it also called a tonic chord?"

"Yes, you have learned a lot from your teacher. Let me write both names."

(I) chord or a tonic chord. Next Mr. Jeffrey wrote a (IV) chord or sub dominant followed by writing a (V) chord or a dominant chord. "Chrissy, will you play those for me?"

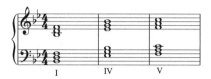

Chrissy played the three chords. "How's that, Mr. Jeffrey?" But, before he could answer, Dale raised his hand.

"I'm confused. What do you mean by tonic and dominant chords?"

"I'll explain in a minute, but for now just listen while I explain this to the piano, drums and bass, the rhythm section." Mr. Jeffrey continued, "The three chords I showed you will provide the base for our first piece. We'll call it a twelve-bar blues progression."

Mr. Jeffrey wrote the chords for the twelve-bar blues progression. "The first four bars just use the (I) chord - **I, I, I, I.** The middle 4 bars go **IV, IV, I, I,** and the last 4 bars go **V, IV, I, V.** Then you repeat the whole thing again.

So, the basic twelve-bar sequence looks like this."

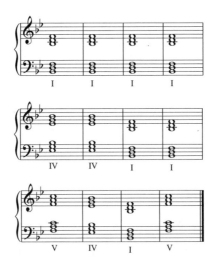

"Chrissy, can you play this progression and make sure you hold out each chord for four counts? Dave, I want you to play on your drums the swing beat you've learned. And, P.J., since you're just learning string bass, I want you to play the root or bottom note of each chord in quarter notes. So P.J., you'll only play three different notes, Bb, Eb, and F."

"I can do three notes. But, you only want me to change the note when the chord changes?"

"Correct, you'll start with Bb on the (I) chord for the entire first line. Then on the second line, you'll change to Eb on the (IV) chord for two bars, followed by F on the (V) chord for the third and fourth bars."

P.J. interrupted. "Don't tell me the third line! Let me try by myself."

Mr. Jeffrey nodded, and P.J. named the remaining notes.

"I think you have it," and Mr. Jeffrey started to snap his fingers in rhythm. "I'll count off to start, and then Chrissy, Dave and P.J. will play that progression or the twelve-bar blues. Ready?" Chrissy sat up with her fingers curved over the keys while Dave readied his drum sticks. Beads of perspiration formed on P.J.'s forehead as he focused on the music. "One, two, ah one, two, three, four."

The three young players played through the twelve bars slowly keeping in time before Mr. Jeffrey stopped them. "Great job! You really stayed together. Remember, you're the rhythm section. It's your job to keep the rhythm steady at all times."

Then the director turned his attention to the other players. "I want Bridget, Karl, Dale, and Bobby to play a Bb concert scale. Remember to transpose the scale just like you do in band. I talk in concert pitch and you think in your key. Bridget, do you remember how?"

"I am in the key of G, so I'll play a G scale." Bridget said without hesitation because she knew she was right.

"Bobby and Dale, your instruments are in the same key, so what will you play?"

Bobby blurted out the answer before Dale could speak. "We're in the key of C, so we'll play the C scale."

"Correct! Karl, yours is easy because you're a C instrument. You'll play in the same key as the concert pitch." Karl was disappointed that he didn't have a chance to show off.

The group played the scale up and down. When they finished, Mr. Jeffrey said, "I've written the scale on the board in concert pitch and put Roman numerals under each note. In band you have played pieces in both major and minor keys. The upper-case Roman numerals (I, IV, V) are major, the lower case (ii, iii) are minor and the seventh note (vii°) is diminished. Don't worry about anything but the major ones for today."

Mr. Jeffrey continued, "Do you notice the number I, IV, and V under the first, fourth, and fifth notes of the scale? Those are the chords I was talking to Chrissy and P.J. about. I want you to play the note of the scale that corresponds to the Roman numeral on the three lines of the twelve-bar blues progression with the rhythm section. Remember P.J. only had to play three notes, and you only need three to start. Hold each one out for four counts."

Dale said, "So when we start, I'll play the first note of my scale (I) four times, once with each measure. Then when the chord changes to a (IV), I'll play my fourth note twice before I go back and play the (I) chord two times, followed by the (V) chord for four counts." Dale continued to explain the rest of the notes he would play.

"Let's try it," Mr. Jeffrey said. "I'll play my cornet while you say your note names. I'll play with one hand and point at the chords with my other hand as they change."

Mr. Jeffrey counted off. "One, two, ah one, two, three, four."

"I got it! Let me try playing now," Karl said jumping up and down.

"OK, the rest of you just say your note names while Karl plays. I'll point at the chords as we go."

When Karl finished, Mr. Jeffrey congratulated the trombonist. "Now let's all play together."

Mr. Jeffrey counted off and the group began playing the chord changes. As soon as they finished doing the twelve bars, Mr. Jeffrey complimented them.

"That's all we'll do for today. Remember, this week we'll meet each day before you graduate on Friday. The best way to learn to play jazz is to listen to recordings. I suggest you go to Swan Records and see if they have the *St. Louis Blues* by W. C. Handy and the *Basin Street Blues* by Spencer Williams. If they do, listen to these pieces before you come to rehearsal tomorrow."

Dale and P.J. helped move the piano back. "I didn't realize that everything we learned in band would relate to jazz. That makes learning jazz easier."

"Easy for you to say! Look at my fingers from playing the bass. I've got big red calluses from all that playing."

Chrissy walked up behind the boys. "Boo hoo! You aren't going to cry, are you?"

Everyone laughed as P.J. realized he was whining. "I guess that's the price I pay for learning a new instrument."

Dale changed the subject. "How about after school we go to Swan's and get the two recordings? Then we can listen to them at my house and practice what we learned. I have a piano that Chrissy can play. Dave, you can play on some pots with your drum sticks."

The group decided to meet at the bike rack after school, and since Chrissy and Bridget walked to school, the boys offered them a ride on the backs of their bikes.

"Dale, I get to ride with you! Bridget, you get Dave, so P.J. can carry the tuba in his duffle bag. I don't think he can carry both a tuba and Bridget at the same time."

P.J. looked relieved as he put the string bass in the back of the auditorium.

"Come on let's get to class. I don't want to get in any trouble my last week of school," Karl said.

After school the gang rode down to the record store. When they asked Mr. Swan if he had any recordings of *St. Louis Blues* and *Basin Street*, he said, "Sure, but what version?"

"There's more than one? Mr. Jeffrey didn't tell us that," Chrissy said.

"Let me explain. The fun part about jazz is there are so many versions and that you have to decide which artist you want. We have several." Mr. Swan went on to explain that he not only had the original recordings that W.C. Handy did of the *Saint Louis Blues* in 1923, but also he had several others, including the Louis Armstrong version with Earl Hines on piano.

Mr. Swan flipped through a bin of records. "If you want the original *Basin Street Blues* by Spencer Williams, I have that one. But, I also have two others, one by Louis Armstrong and The Hot Five and one by the trombonist Jack Teagarden and the Charleston Chasers. Both songs have lyrics."

"They have words?" Bobby said.

"Most of the blues songs from that period of time have lyrics. That's what gives the blues its heart and soul."

"You mean this *Heart and Soul*," and Dave sang the melody.

"No, I meant the words give the song feelings and emotion heard and felt in the blues."

Karl said, "Did you say a trombonist recorded *Basin Street Blues*? We want that one for sure."

"OK, but I recommend the W. C. Handy recording of the *Saint Louis Blues*. It'll give you a better idea of how the piece originally sounded. Shall I wrap them up?"

Dale glanced at Bridget. "I don't think we thought about

the money part. I was just so excited..." Karl said as his voice trailed off.

Chrissy whispered to Bridget who nodded her head. She then turned to face Mr. Swan and the boys.

"Bridget and I will make a deal with you. If we pay for the records with our baby sitting money, you have to take us to your fort and the rope swing in the Jungle."

"You also have to take Sandra. She's part of the deal," Bridget said,

"But we don't allow just anyone to go to the fort, especially girls," P.J. said emphatically.

"Give us a minute to talk," Dale said, pulling the boys aside. "If we take them one time, and one time only, we'll be able to get the records and listen to the jazz. And, if not, well, I don't know about you, but I don't have any money. What do you say?"

After several minutes of whispering, and glancing back and forth at he girls, Mr. Swan tapped the counter and said, "Come on, I have other customers."

Dale looked Chrissy in the eye. "You drive a hard bargain. We'll take you. But, only once, and you have to promise not to tell anyone where the fort or the swing are. Promise?"

Chrissy moved closer. "Sandra also, right?"

"Yes! Now swear!"

The girls put their right hands over their hearts. "Cross my heart and hope to die, stick a needle in my eye not to tell anyone else about the fort or the swing."

"Good ... Mr. Swan, wrap 'em up," Dale said.

"Can you throw in the piano sheet music?" Chrissy said pulling out her wallet. "I want to practice reading the original music before we improvise."

After making their purchase, everyone rode to the fire station to get the dogs. The ride to Dale's house was faster than usual, since they were really eager to play the records and start practicing.

Chapter 16

SURPRISE

Grandma sat down next to Dale at breakfast the next morning. "I haven't had that much fun in years," Grandma said.

"Me, too! Thanks for having the gang for dinner. I can't believe that we practiced until almost ten o'clock last night. You'd think I'd be tired, but I'm not. Practicing jazz got me going."

"I'll have to say you're right," Grandma replied and she looked past Dale as if she saw something in the distance. "I haven't sung *Basin Street Blues* in years. That sure brought back some memories."

"Do you believe that we could learn that piece by ear after listening to it on the record player? It was really great that you helped Chrissy with the piano part so we could hear the chords. I like playing by ear."

"I enjoyed it, too," and she picked up Dale's empty oatmeal dish. "I'll bet Mr. Jeffrey will be surprised at what you learned in one rehearsal."

"The plan is that we'll be playing *Basin Street* when he walks in."

"Ride carefully with Chrissy on the back of your bike," grandma said as Dale breezed out the door. "I don't want any broken bones."

"Right on time," Chrissy said as she hopped on the seat of his bike. "I heard you whistle for Scout and knew you would be coming."

As Dale coasted the bike down Simpson Hill, Chrissy tightened her grip around Dale's waist and stuck her legs out.

"Your grandmother can sure play the piano and sing."

"I was surprised that she could sing, too! I also didn't know that when your parents came over to walk you home that they knew the words to the song, too."

As they turned onto Main Street they could see the entire gang waiting with Bridget on the back of Victor's bike and P.J. with his tuba on his back.

"Dale, do you think you could do a skid with me on the back. I hear you guys talking about your skids. Wouldn't it be fun to do one together? They'd never expect it."

"If you hang on real tight and lean in the same direction as I do, then we can do it. Let me pick up some speed and when I lean, you lean. Ready?" Dale said as he stood up and started pedaling faster in a beeline toward the gang.

"How come Dale's going so fast? Isn't he getting kind of close?" Bridget tightened her grip on Victor. "Is he going to hit us?" Bridget said as she started to get off Victor's bike.

"I know what they're going to do. Just stay on the bike and act like you are not scared," Victor said.

"Not be scared?" But, before Victor could answer, Dale hit the brakes, and both he and Chrissy leaned to the right. The rubber tires made a loud scraping sound on the pavement as the bike came to a halt at Bridget's feet.

"Got yah!" Dale said.

Bridget, exasperated, frowned red and forcefully put her hands on her hips. Everyone, including Chrissy, started laughing.

"I told you to pretend not to be scared. I knew Dale would do that. He does it every morning, but I've never seen a double-person skid."

"Victor, do not even think about trying that with me on the back."

"I won't—maybe," he said as he pushed off and led the way to school with a sly grin on his face. As they ran up the sidewalk, Mr. Malone was unlocking the main entrance door. "What are you doing here so early?"

P.J. was the first in the door. "We came early to surprise Mr. Jeffrey with a song we learned last night. Is it alright if we go to the auditorium and get ready?"

Mr. Malone stroked his chin. "Since you're sixth graders, I should be able to trust you. What's the song?"

"*Basin Street Blues.* Do you know it?" Chrissy said.

Mr. Malone started walking down the hall toward the auditorium snapping his fingers in tempo. After a few steps, he turned toward the kids, and sang in a soft voice, "Won't cha come along with me?"

Won't cha come   a long   with me,

Followed by the gang singing back, "Down that Mississippi."

Down   that Mis   sis   sip   pi?

He answered back, "We'll take a boat to the land of dreams."

we'll take_   a boat   to   the   land   of dreams

The gang answered, "Come along with me on, down to New Orleans."

come a long with me on down to   ne w Or leans

Everyone laughed as the janitor unlocked the door, "Thanks for letting us in. You sing great."

"You're welcome. Do you know what it's called when one person sings one phrase and another one answers?"

No one answered.

"Where I come from, it's a call-and-response. Ask Mr. Jeffrey. He'll tell you more." As Mr. Malone went down the hall, the gang could hear him singing the next verse.

Now the band's there to greet us
Old friends will meet us
Where all them folks going to the St. Louis Cemetery
meet Heaven on earth.... they call it Basin Street

Once onstage, Bobby put his clarinet together, wetting his reed before warming up. Chrissy moved the piano to the front of the stage, and the group tuned. Then they sat quietly, waiting for Mr. Jeffrey. The door in the back of the auditorium flung open, and Mr. Malone popped his head in. "He's just coming in the building. How about if I turn off the lights? Do you think you can play in the dark? That way he won't know who's playing until he turns on the lights."

"Go ahead and turn off the lights," Chrissy said. The stage went black.

"I'll count us off like Mr. Jeffrey does. Ready, one, two a one two three," and the group started playing.

When they were on the third verse, the lights flickered on. Mr. Prenty stood just inside the auditorium with his mouth wide open. Just behind him were Mr. Jeffrey and Mrs. Cooper. The group finished playing and when they stopped they yelled, "Surprise!"

At first, the three adults did not move. Then, Mr. Jeffrey brushed past the principal and walked quickly down the aisle of the auditorium to the edge of the stage, followed by Mr. Prenty and Mrs. Cooper.

Bobby couldn't wait any longer. "Are you angry?"

"At first we were furious when we thought someone had broken into the auditorium until we turned on the lights. Now, though, I think we're shocked. We can't believe that you worked this song out on your own." Mr. Jeffrey started to clap and the other two adults joined him. Then he leaned on his hands and lifted himself onto the stage.

"As long as you're here early, let's start rehearsal. We'll take what you learned and tweak it. Now play the first two lines."

When the group stopped, Karl said, "Mr. Malone told us this was called a call-and-response."

"He's right. That's when you hear a solo part followed by the rest of the musicians repeating the same phrase. Knowing the structure makes you play the song with more understanding."

During the last half of the rehearsal Mr. Jeffrey taught the group the chord progression for *St. Louis Blues*. At the end of rehearsal, the group decided to meet at Chrissy's house after school and listen to the recording and practice.

As Mr. Jeffrey put his music away, he warned, "This has been a great rehearsal but please don't come early tomorrow!"

Chapter 17

FIRSTS AND LASTS

Dale woke up extra early to get his P.T. in with Scout. Today he would meet the gang at the fire station for their last ride to Emerson School. He would get his report card, and summer vacation would finally begin.

Dale was pacing himself to make the climb up Simpson Hill when Scout, who usually trotted next to him, ran a few feet ahead of him. The fur on the back of Scout's neck stood up and his ears were perked. As the dog ran, he kept sweeping his head, sniffing the air.

"What's the matter, boy?"

Scout didn't look back at Dale. Instead, he let out a low growl as they turned into the alley behind the Kingston home. Scout was within sight of the garage, when he came to a sudden stop. Dale caught up, breathing hard, and knelt down beside Scout. "Why are you acting so strange, Scout? Do you want me to...," and before he could finish the sentence, Jim Petris and four of his friends stepped out from the bushes that lined the alley. Scout bared his teeth and emitted a throaty growl. He crouched down and took a few steps toward the boys.

"Call your dog off!" Jim shouted taking a step back.

"Scout, come!" Dale commanded, but the dog, his eyes locked on Jim, kept moving slowly toward the group.

Before Dale could get a hold of Scout's collar, Jim turned and ran to a tree. Just as he grabbed onto a limb, Scout lunged forward and jumped, grabbing ahold of Jim's back pocket with his teeth. Scout shook his head and ripped the material before Jim was able to hoist himself up onto the branch. His friends followed suit, barely escaping before Scout turned on them.

"Scout, get over here!" but Scout ignored Dale. He clawed the tree trunk, barking ferociously and snapping at the boys' feet that were dangling overhead.

Dale finally caught up to Scout and pulled him back, "Settle down, Scout! Settle down!" Scout stopped barking but the dog kept his eyes focused on the boys in the tree.

"I don't think he likes you for some reason. What are you doing here so early?"

"It's none of your business what we're doing here, and I don't think you'd be so tough if you didn't have that dog with you," Jim said from the tree causing Scout to growl and pull away from Dale.

"Well, I don't think you'd be so tough if you didn't always have your friends with you," Dale said fiercely not wanting to show he was afraid.

"We'll see who the tough one is when you get to junior high."

Dale pulled Scout away from the tree. "I think they know better than to mess with us." This time Scout obeyed his master and turned to run alongside Dale while looking back toward the boys who had jumped out of the tree. They sprinted down the alley toward Simpson Hill.

When they got to the garage, Scout sat down next to Dale and looked up. "Good dog! Thanks for protecting me. You learned a lot from Dogs for Defense!" Dale said as he scratched Scout's fur.

"I don't know what his problem is, but he sure doesn't like me. Either way, you sure scared him, didn't you?"

Dale's mother was at the kitchen table when Dale came in. Dale sat down and took a swig of his coffee. He took a rusk off the plate and buttered it as he sat lost in thought. Mom glanced over at him.

"How come you're so quiet this morning? Anything going on?"

"No … I'm just thinking about my last day at Emerson."

Mother stood and took her dishes to the sink. "Hmmm… don't forget to give Mrs. Cooper her present," and she pointed to the jar of strawberry preserves sitting on the counter.

Dale excused himself and left the kitchen to dress for school. When he returned, grandmother had his lunch ready.

"Be careful not to break that jar on your way to school," grandma said as Dale disappeared through the door and whistled for Scout.

As Dale rode to the fire station, he cautiously looked down each cross street. Even Scout seemed to be on high alert. By the time they reached the bottom of Simpson Hill, Dale began to relax and think about his last day at Emerson. The past seven years had seemed to fly by and now he was finally going to graduate and start a new adventure at a new school. As Dale turned onto Main Street, he could see the gang sitting on the curb in front of the fire station chatting away. Scout took off to meet Smokey and Dale rode faster preparing for a great skid right in front of the gang. At the last instance, Dale slammed on his brakes leaving a trail of black rubber that ended at the boys' feet. The only one to jump out of the way was P.J. while the rest of the boys trusted Dale's ability to stop in time.

"That beats all the others," Karl said admiring the mark. On the pavement each boy had skidded to a stop trying to beat each other's as they arrived at the station but Dale's was by far the best.

P.J. offered to tie up the dogs, while Dale sat down on the curb with the others.

Dave said, "Can we take our time today and enjoy our last ride?"

"OK, but let's ride no hands! It'll be more fun," Bobby said.

P.J. returned, and the gang jumped on their bikes and rode off. Riding in a group without any hands was a real challenge. In order to keep their balance, they would swerve back and forth, almost bumping into one another. When the boys arrived at the bike rack, Chrissy, Sandra, and Bridget were sitting on their bikes with ruck sacks on, just like the boys.

Dale was the last one to pull up to the rack.

"How come you were the last one? You're usually the first?" Chrissy said with a big smile.

"I promised grandma I wouldn't break the jar of preserves she made for Mrs. Cooper. If I'd crashed and broken it, I would've been in big trouble."

"I brought Mrs. Cooper a scarf I knitted," Bridget said proudly, followed by each one telling what gift they had for their teacher on this last day of school.

"We can't wait to go to the Jungle today after we get our report cards!" Sandra said.

"I don't see how you're going to get through all the weeds and brush with those skirts on," Bobby said.

"Even though we can't wear pants to school, we can wear them afterward." Sandra undid the drawstring of her rucksack and pulled out a pair of pants. "We packed jeans and our gym shoes, and we'll change right after class. Don't worry about us slowing you down. We can handle ourselves in the woods."

"Enough talk! I don't want to be late my last day," Dale said.

The gang was still talking and laughing as they entered Mrs. Cooper's room. After placing the gifts on her desk, they took their seats as the bell rang.

"I understand your excitement this morning, but we do have a few things to take care of before I hand out the report cards and you can leave. First, thanks for all of the lovely gifts. I'll miss you all and wish you luck next year at the junior high," and she quickly dabbed her eye with an embroidered handkerchief she took from her pocket. She proudly smiled at the class as she bent down to get something out of her drawer.

"At the beginning of the school year, I made a promise to Dale." Chrissy raised her eyebrows and quizzically looked over at Dale. Mrs. Cooper continued, "I told Dale that I would play my flute for the class, if he didn't work on his music during my class. He kept his part of the bargain, and now I'll keep mine." The teacher held up a beautiful silver flute with a gold head joint just as Mrs. Vincent, the general music teacher, entered and sat down at the piano.

"I want to perform a short selection I think you've heard. It's called *Flight of the Bumble Bee* by Rimsky-Korsakov. The fastest I've ever played has been one minute." She walked down the row and stood next to Dale's desk. "Take this stopwatch and time me. Let's see if I can beat my own record."

Dale knew how to use a stopwatch from timing students in Mr. Cabutti's gym class during the annual fifty-yard dash fitness test.

"Do you want me to start on your first note?"

"First let me play a few notes to warm up." Mrs. Cooper played a few long tones, scales, and tuned to the piano before she turned back to Dale. "Start the watch on my first note."

Slowly Mrs. Cooper brought the flute up to her lips and a silence fell over the room. Mrs. Cooper took a quick breath, and with a nod of her head, she started. Dale clicked the button of the stopwatch.

The students were on the edges of their chairs listening to the piano and flute race through the notes. Dale concentrated on the hand of the stopwatch as the seconds ticked by and Mrs. Cooper took her final breath and plunged into the last phrase.

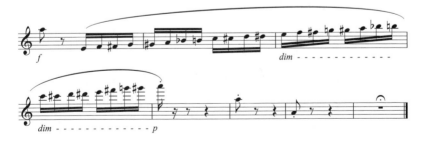

At the final note, Dale stopped the watch and stared at the time.

Mrs. Cooper brought her flute down. "Well? Did I break my own record?"

Dale smiled broadly and showed the watch to the class. "Fifty-four seconds! You beat your old record by six seconds!"

The class erupted in applause and shouts of "Bravo!" Just then, the door flung open and Mr. Prenty burst through.

"What's all this commotion?"

Mrs. Cooper raised her hand to silence the students and explained her feat to the principal.

Mr. Prenty didn't look impressed. "Well, just remember that school's not finished yet."

The principal disappeared through the door just as quickly as he had appeared. Mrs. Cooper lifted her flute over her head in celebration, and put a finger to her lips signaling the students to be silent.

"I hope you enjoyed seeing your teacher get in trouble, but it was worth it. Let me put my instrument away and get my list out. I want to check off one of my items."

"You have a list?" Dale said with surprise.

"After catching P.J. with his list, I started my own." Taking a piece of paper from her desk she took out a pencil. "Item number four. Beat my old record for playing *Flight of the Bumble Bee*. Done! Now only eight to go."

The class began to clap, but Mrs. Cooper quieted them. "I don't want Mr. Prenty to come back" she said, with a gentle look on her face.

One by one, Mrs. Cooper called everyone up to her desk and handed the student a report card. When the last name was called, she thanked them again for a great year and dismissed the class. The gang stood around the teacher's desk, talking, and laughing, before leaving the room for the final time. By the time they got to the bike rack, Bridget, Sandra, and Chrissy wearing their jeans, gyms shoes, and t-shirts were waiting for them.

"Now do we look like we're ready for the Jungle?" Bridget said. "What is it that you guys always say? Let's race?" The gang, that now included the girls, jumped on their bikes and began racing through the streets of Libertyville toward the Jungle.

As the group neared the end of the block where the trail to the Jungle began, Victor raced ahead to claim the win. Dale was second, and Bridget was third.

After taking a deep breath, Dale said. "Before we take you into the Jungle, you have to promise never to bring anyone here again. And, this is the only time you get to come here with us."

"We promise," Sandra said, inching her bike toward the trail. "Now let's go!"

Tommy led the way down the path through the brush. Over the hills and down through the creek they rode until they finally reached the fort. P.J. swung his leg over his bike and hopped off. "What do you think?"

"It's better than I imagined with all the camouflage netting," Chrissy said admiringly as she walked up to the structure. "What's on the top? Is that a trap door to the roof with a flag?"

"Come on inside," Dale said leading the way.

"You have helmets and binoculars? Where'd you get them?" Bridget said putting a helmet on her head.

"General Packston gave them to us for saving the Air Force base from the fire. Pretty neat, huh?" P. J. said.

Sandra poked around in the corner of the fort. "Why do these buckets have dirt clods?"

"Those are for hand grenades when we play Capture the Flag. They bust apart and leave dust and pieces of dirt everywhere when we throw them," Dave said heaving a clod so it exploded right next to Bridget. She dusted off her jeans, giving Dave a dirty look.

"Can we play a game of Capture the Flag?" Chrissy said.

"I don't know. We have to sweep out the spiders, collect some new dirt clods and find sticks for guns. Let's get the chores done first," Bobby said.

The girls pitched in sweeping and gathering the new dirt clods. In no time, the fort was ready for an afternoon of fun. "Can we eat now?" P.J. said rubbing his stomach.

"Let's eat on the roof. That way the girls can see what it's like from up there," Dale said.

The group climbed the ladder and sat in the warm

afternoon sun. They reminisced about their favorite grade school memory. The breeze was cool as it blew through the large oak that hung over the fort's roof. After much laughter Chrissy said, "Well, what do you think? Can we play the game?"

"I don't know," Victor said shaking his head. "I can think of three reasons why you can't. One, you'll get dirty, two, you throw like a girl, and since you've never played before, you'd be too easy to shoot."

"We don't care about getting dirty," Sandra said emphatically, and she poked Victor in the shoulder. "And, what do you mean that we're too easy to shoot and we throw like girls?" Her face turned red and her voice was getting louder.

Dale interrupted, "I've got an idea. I'll take the girls on my team, since I'm the one who let them come here in the first place. We'll have three teams. Victor, Bobby, and Dave will be one team that will defend the area around the fort. Tommy, Karl, and P.J. with Smokey will defend the fort from the inside. I'll take Sandra, Bridget, and Chrissy with Scout and we'll attack the fort to capture the flag. Does that sound fair?"

The boys looked at each other before answering. "There's no way, Dale, that your team can beat us. This'll be easy," Victor said smugly.

"Do you want to bet something?" Bridget said with a challenging tone in her voice.

"Like what?"

"How about if we win, we can come with you whenever we want for the rest of the summer? If we lose, we'll give you the records we bought and not come back to the fort again."

Victor turned to his team for a short discussion. "That seems pretty fair to me," he observed.

"Alright, it's settled," and Victor, Tommy, and Bridget shook hands.

"Victor, you have the watch. Give us fifteen minutes. When the time is up, whistle to start the game," Dale said.

The time began, and Dale and the girls grabbed a bucket of dirt clods, selected some sticks that looked like guns and took off down the trail with Scout. At the first clearing, Dale explained the rules about not throwing dirt clods at anyone's head, especially P. J.'s. He also demonstrated how to make shooting sounds. "Now let's make a plan of attack."

Bridget spoke first. "I've got an idea. They think we can't throw or that we don't want to get dirty, so we should use that to our advantage."

"Are you sure you don't mind getting muddy?"

"We don't mind. Especially if we can defeat them," Chrissy said with excitement.

"First, we need to get someone on the roof to get the flag. They'll expect us to stay together and not break up, so Chrissy and Bridget should go down the trail until you get to the creek. Once you get to the creek, turn right and follow it behind the fort. Crawl along the bank on the right. The water is noisy, the bank is steep and they won't look over the edge. It's really muddy and they won't expect it. Once you get to the fort, Bridget, you go to the north side of the fort and wait. There aren't any windows on that side. When you hear me whistle, and Scout starts barking, come out of the creek and climb up the side of the fort using the old ladder leaning against the side. That ladder's from the old fort and they won't remember it. Chrissy, when she gets out of the creek and starts to climb, you throw some clods through the back window. Don't stop until Bridget has the flag. Do you understand?"

"I can't wait to see their faces when we win," Chrissy said, smiling at Dale.

"We haven't won yet," Dale said.

"What am I supposed to do?" Sandra asked, feeling left out of the plan.

"You'll come with me because you're a good thrower. Also, we can use the double tongue sound to make shooting sounds. They'll think it's me and never think that we both can make that sound. Scout will come with us, and we'll work our way up to the front. We can tie some brush on Scout and send him off running, raising a bunch of dust. They'll think it's us and give chase. Sandra, when they run by shoot them, using the TA-KA-TA-KA sound. Then when they're shot, start throwing clods in the front window. With both of you throwing from the front and the back, they'll keep their heads down. I'll rush the front and help Bridget up the ladder if needed."

Just as Dale finished discussing the plan, Victor gave a long high whistle to signal the game had started.

"Keep quiet and good luck!" The two groups split up and put the plan in action.

When Bridget and Chrissy got to the creek they crawled along the bank in the mud toward the fort. They could hear the boys above them, moving back and forth through the weeds looking for them. Chrissy held up her muddy hand to her mouth and made the SHH signal to Bridget before they continued crawling up the creek. When they made it to the back of the fort, they looked up. Staring at them from the edge was Smokey. The dog just looked at the two mud-covered girls with his tail wagging.

Chrissy reached into her back pocket and took out a cookie she had saved from lunch. She slowly raised her muddy hand showing Smokey the cookie and motioning for him to come get it. Smokey did not hesitate and came down the bank to the girls. Smokey happily gobbled the cookie, not giving away their position. In the meantime, Sandra and Dale crawled through the thick brush and dirt until they were within twenty yards of the fort. Dale took off his belt and attached it to Scout with some dead branches tucked in. Sandra readied her dirt clods and licked her lips, getting ready to use the double tongue sound to shoot the boys when they ran past. Dale gave Sandra, whose face was covered in dust, a thumbs-up and whispered in Scout's ear. Scout took off running and barking, raising a large dust cloud.

"There they are. ATTACK!" Victor said leading Bobby and Dave toward the dust.

Upon hearing the commotion, Bridget jumped out of the creek and raced to the side of the fort as Chrissy hurled a dirt grenade through the back window. It landed with a thud against the side of the fort. The boys inside tossed dirt clods back but the clods flew harmlessly over her head. Victor, Dave, and Bobby were about to start shooting when Sandra jumped up in front of them making the TA-KA sound. Once they realized they were out of the game, Sandra picked up her dirt grenades and threw them through the front window with such force that they made a huge smacking sound as they hit the wall inside. Bridget was so muddy she nearly slipped as she climbed the ladder. As she climbed higher, she felt it start to slide off the side of the fort. She looked down to see Dale run under the cover of Sandra's dirt clods and grab the ladder to steady it. Bridget resumed her climb to the roof. Inside, the boys could hear her climbing. P.J. tried to run to the inside ladder to stop her, but the dirt clods flying through the windows forced him to hit the floor for cover.

Bridget hoisted herself onto the roof and grabbed the flag from the pole. "We won, we won!" The other teams emerged from inside the fort and the surrounding area with their hands up in surrender. Bridget climbed back down the ladder to congratulate her team. The boys looked in admiration at the muddy, dusty girls standing next to Dale, as Scout wagged his tail with the branches still attached to him.

"Do you still think we throw like girls?" Sandra said, putting her hands on her hips, standing as tall as she could.

Victor admitted defeat. "You won fair and square. You can come to the Jungle any time you want, and I think the girls should be divided up so they're not all on the same team," and all the boys nodded approvingly and in agreement.

"Let's try out Tommy's swing we've heard so much about," Chrissy said gingerly.

The gang took off running for the quarry. Tommy demonstrated and explained how to let go when the rope was as far out over the water as possible. Chrissy wanted to go first and grabbed the rope from Tommy's hand. She ran as fast as she could, swung out over the water, letting go with a scream of delight. When she hit the water, the mud from her clothes made a brown pool where she hit the water. Each one took turns swinging and swimming in the cool water. Afterwards, they lay on the cool granite rocks enjoying the warm afternoon sun, talking rapidly about school and the summer ahead.

Chrissy, who was lying next to Dale, sat up. Looking Dale square in the eye she gently said, "Thanks for letting us come here today. What a great way to start our summer!"

Before anyone could join in, the Conn factory whistle blew in the distance, signaling that it was time to head home.

Chapter 18

MEMORIAL DAY

Dale and his grandfather had been practicing for two weeks for the annual Memorial Day ceremony. They had been asked to play *Taps* and the echo. Echo *Taps* is when one player stands by the memorial and the second player remains out of sight from the crowd. After the first player plays the opening phrase, the second player repeats (echoes) it back. As the second player, Dale had to time his phrase just right so it sounded like an echo. This past week, Dale and his grandfather practiced at the cemetery just out of town. They found a place for Dale to stand where he would not be seen but the sound from his bugle would be easy to hear. Today's ceremony on May 30, 1945, would be a very special one since the war in Europe had just ended on May 8, and the country was putting all of its efforts into the war against Japan that was still raging in the Pacific.

On the day of the ceremony, Dale and his grandfather sat at the kitchen table eating breakfast while Dale looked at a program.

"How come on the program there are two names for the ceremony? One is Decoration Day and the other is Memorial Day."

"Originally it was called Decoration Day because during the Civil War, the story goes that the women's groups in the South decorated the Confederate graves to honor those who had died in battle. In 1886, May 30 was officially proclaimed as a day to remember both Union and Confederate soldiers at Arlington National Cemetery in Washington, D.C. by placing flowers on their graves. After World War I, the ceremony changed from just honoring Civil War casualties to honoring all military personnel who died regardless of what war."

"How do you know all of this?"

"Remember, son, I was a bugle player and have played many a funeral and Memorial Day ceremony. In order to appreciate and understand the importance of these events, you have to understand the history that surrounds it."

"That's what Mr. Jeffrey says about the songs we play in band and at the concerts. He says you can't understand how to properly play a piece if you don't know the history or the story behind the music."

Grandpa nodded his head. "If you look at today's program, you'll see the high school choir is going to sing the hymn, *Kneel Where Our Loves Are Sleeping.*"

"Why'd they pick that?"

"Well, that's where the history comes in. It was written right after the Civil War ended and you can see in the program that it was dedicated 'To the Ladies of the South who are decorating the graves of the Confederate Dead.' So if you know the history regarding Decoration Day, then you understand the meaning of the song and the words."

Dale studied the program and then asked. "What's the meaning of this poem?"

"I feel like this is a test," grandpa said and he chuckled. "But I do know the answer. During the First World War, a young officer wrote a poem to commemorate not only his friend's death, but also the thousands of other soldiers who died fighting in that horrible war. After it was published, a young woman wrote a poem in reply. She was the first to start the tradition of selling red poppies to honor our veterans and to raise money to help service men in need."

In Flanders Fields by John McCrae, May 1915

In Flanders fields the poppies blow
Between the crosses, row on row,
That mark our place; and in the sky
The larks, still bravely singing, fly
Scarce heard amid the guns below.

We are the Dead. Short days ago
We lived, felt dawn, saw sunset glow,
Loved and were loved, and now we lie
In Flanders fields.
Take up our quarrel with the foe:
To you from failing hands we throw
The torch; be yours to hold it high.
If ye break faith with us who die
We shall not sleep, though poppies grow
 In Flanders fields.

Monica Michael's poem in response to *In Flanders Fields*, 1915

We cherish too, the poppy red
That grows on fields where valor led,
It seems to signal to the skies
That blood of heroes never dies

"It's amazing the history about a simple ceremony. What happened to the guy that wrote *Flanders Fields*?"

"This was McCrae's only poem. He died in 1918 during the war, but not from battle wounds. Like so many others, he died from pneumonia."

Dale finished his breakfast, vowing to play well to honor all the people who had given their lives for their county.

"Come on, Dale, get your bugle. We don't want to be late."

Dale and his grandfather drove the short distance to the cemetery. By the time they arrived, the graves of the soldiers had flowers and flags placed on them. The VFW was selling poppies and organizing the seven soldiers who would present the twenty-one gun salute. The high school choir was moving onto the risers and Pastor Bob was paging through his script for the service.

The pastor looked up and greeted the Kingstons. "Good morning, C.H. It's a beautiful day for a ceremony," he said, gazing up at the clear blue sky.

"Dale and I will warm up. Will you start at nine o'clock as planned?"

"Yes. That will give you about fifteen minutes. Dale, since you won't be able to see us, wait until you hear me read *Flanders Fields* followed by the twenty-one gun salute. Then C. H. will play taps first, followed by your echo."

Dale and his grandfather walked over to the place where Dale would play the echo to warm up.

They played some lip slurs and long tones. When they were finished, grandpa gave him some advice. "The ceremony may take a while, so go ahead and buzz your lips to stay warmed up. You're far enough away that no one will hear you buzzing. Before you play *Taps,* take a deep breath and relax. Let's make this a memorable performance for all the people here today."

Grandfather shook Dale's hand and headed back over the hill to the ceremony.

The morning sun felt warm on Dale's face as he waited to play. He thought about the history of this day and of all the servicemen and women who had given their lives for their country. Dale turned his head when he heard the choir sing the hymn, and he knew from the program that *Flanders Fields* was next. When the singing stopped Dale licked his lips and began softly buzzing while thinking of each phrase of *Taps* and the pitches he needed to remember. Suddenly, the quiet morning air was shattered by three volleys of rifle fire. Dale was shocked by the how loud the rifles were. He had never heard seven rifles fired at such a close range, let alone three times in unison. As the rifle fire faded, he heard Grandpa play the first phrase of *Taps*, but he froze and could not remember his first note.

What'll happen if I don't answer? Dale thought. In the back of his mind he heard his grandfather's voice. *Take a deep breath and relax.*

As the last note of his grandfather's phrase faded, Dale put the bugle to his lips. He took another deep breath and out came the notes clear and strong. For the next several minutes the two buglers traded phrases until Dale played the last echo. When Dale finished, he stood out of sight of the crowd with hot tears running down his face. Never before had he thought about his own father dying in battle. *How would he ever be able to handle it if his father did not come back from the war?*

Chapter 19

SANDRA

Sandra could not believe that today was going to be her first flight in an airplane. For the past month, Mrs. Kingston, Dale's mom, who was a pilot in the Women's Air Force Service Pilots (WASP), had come to Sandra's house and taught her about airplanes. She believed that anyone can ride in a plane, but to truly enjoy these magnificent machines, a person had to understand what made them work as well as their long history.

Sandra enjoyed reading about history and had read every book she could about early women aviators. She devoured books about Madame Therese Peltier who was the first woman to fly an airplane solo in 1908 and Harriet Quimby, the first American woman to earn a pilot's license, fly at night, and pilot her own aircraft across the English Channel. She was fascinated by the women who were early pioneers of aviation, but the woman she loved reading about most was Amelia

Earhart. She read about her first flight in 1920 with pilot Frank Hawks and her saying afterwards, "By the time I had gotten two to three hundred feet into the air, I knew I had to learn to fly." Sandra hoped her first flight would be as exciting.

Sandra related to Amelia because she, too, was a tom boy who liked to climb trees and could out run the boys. She enjoyed reading about her accomplishments from getting her pilot's license to buying her own bi-plane in 1921 nicknamed *Canary*. Sandra could not believe that she was the first woman to fly solo across both the Atlantic and Pacific Oceans. But, the most interesting flight was her last flight at age forty. While attempting to fly around the world in 1937, she disappeared over the Pacific. Sandra talked to Mrs. Kingston about the flight and her disappearance.

"Aviators such as Amelia Earhart, Nancy Harkness Love and Jackie Cochran have always challenged themselves and their planes to go farther and faster. These great female aviators often gave their lives, attempting to further women's roles in aviation. Because of them, we have the 99 Club, an organization dedicated to furthering women's role in flight. We also have the WASP pilots flying military aircraft. Flight does involve risk, and we must always follow the strict guidelines for flying. As my first flight instructor taught me, 'There are old pilots and there are bold pilots, but there are no old, bold pilots.' This is why we follow the rules and try and make flight as safe as possible. That's why I want to teach you about planes and what pilots do, so that you can really appreciate flight."

Several weeks ago, Sandra had asked Mrs. Kingston, "What type of plane will we fly in?"

"Your first flight should be in the same kind of plane all military pilots fly in the first time, a Stearman N2S bi-plane nicknamed 'The Yellow Peril.' It's a two-seater and has an open cockpit with dual controls."

"What do you mean by open?"

"Just what it sounds like. We'll have a little glass windshield in front of our faces but nothing else. You'll be able to feel the rush of air over the plane's open cockpit and the singing vibration of the engine and bracing wires in flight."

"So if I look over the side or straight up, there won't be anything around me?"

"That's right! All you'll have is a harness to hold you in your seat, a leather hat, goggles, leather jacket, and a parachute."

"A parachute?"

"Yes, because this plane is able to do aerobatic maneuvers and that requires the pilot and passenger to wear parachutes in case they have to get out in an emergency. Remember what I said about safety? We don't take any chances, so if something goes wrong, we can get back down safely. Don't worry, Sandra, I've flown thousands of hours and haven't had to jump out yet in an emergency."

For the next two weeks Sandra learned all the names of the parts of the airplane and what they did. She learned how the rubber pedals, joy stick, throttle, trim tabs and flaps were used to control the plane in flight. Sandra got a diagram of the plane and the plane's specifications. Mrs. Kingston said all pilots have to understand each plane's specifications and limitations so she can fly the plane correctly. Each plane is different and until you understand what the plane can and cannot do, you can't be certified to fly it.

Boeing N2S Stearman--The Yellow Peril
Aircraft Specifications

Specifications:	Boeing N2S Stearman
Engine:.	One 220-horsepower Continental R-670-5 piston radial engine
Empty Weight:	1,936 lbs.
Max Takeoff Weight: . . .	2,717 lbs.
Wing Span:	32 ft. 2 in.
Length:	24 ft. 3 in.
Height:	9 ft. 2 in.
Maximum Speed:	124 mph
Ceiling:	11,200 ft.
Range:	505 miles
Armament:	None

"Sandra, you'll make a tremendous pilot because you have all the qualities a pilot needs. You're smart, organized, strong, and most important, you follow rules."

Sandra looked at all of the pictures of planes in her books and the famous pilots on her bedroom walls and took a deep breath.

"Today will be one of my greatest adventures ever," she said, pulling back her hair into a pony tail and putting on her leather flight jacket. She went downstairs to meet Mrs. Kingston at ten o'clock sharp. As she got to the bottom of the stairs, her mom was waiting for her.

"You look ready to go, but you're missing something."

"I am? I have my leather flight cap, goggles, and gloves. No, I think I have it all."

"Dale dropped this by this morning and said all good pilots have them."

"What is it?" she said taking the long thin box from her mom.

"Open it and find out. He said he made it."

Sandra opened the box to find a white silk scarf with the letter S embroidered in black thread. Letting out a scream, she said, "This is just like the one Errol Flynn wears in his movies."

After her mom tied the scarf around her neck, Sandra looked in the mirror. "This scarf makes the whole outfit look great." But, before her mom could answer, Sandra heard a horn honk. Mrs. Kingston was waiting outside in the Jeep.

"Bye, Mom! Be sure to go outside when you hear a plane. Mrs. Kingston said we would fly over the house so I could see what it looks like from the air."

"I'll be waiting and be careful," she said with worry in her voice.

Sandra was out the door and into the Jeep in seconds.

"My, my, look at you with the scarf and everything."

"Dale gave me the scarf. Did he really embroider my initial?"

"Yes, he knew I had one, so he thought you should also. It's not the best embroidery you'll ever see."

"I think it's fabulous!"

The drive to the Air Force base took about ten minutes, and after checking with the guard at the main gate, they drove to the hangar where the plane was parked. Once inside, two soldiers helped Sandra and Mrs. Kingston put on their parachutes.

"Look at how beautiful the plane is! The pictures I have are nothing compared to the real thing."

"Follow me and I'll do the pre-flight walk around and explain why we do it." For the next few minutes, Sandra walked with Mrs. Kingston and mimicked what she did. They ran their hands on the leading edges of the wings, inspected the rudder and flaps, tested the guide wires and checked the tires to make sure they were inflated correctly. The last thing they checked was the fuel. First, Mrs. Kingston opened the fuel cap and looked inside to make sure it was full, followed by taking a long test tube and draining some of the fuel into it to make sure there was no moisture in the fuel.

"Do all pilots have to walk around and inspect the plane before flying?"

"Yes, it's a pilot's responsibility to make sure the airplane is safe and in proper working order. Climb in, and I'll do the cockpit preflight, and then we will be off."

The two soldiers who had assisted them with the parachutes helped Sandra into the front seat while Mrs. Kingston climbed in the back seat. They strapped her in and made sure she understood how to get out of the seat harness and the airplane in case of an emergency. Next, they showed her how to pull the rip cord that would open the chute after getting out of the plane. The last thing they did was help her adjust her leather hat that contained her ear phones and mike, so she could hear and talk to Mrs. Kingston during the flight.

"Sandra, can you hear me? Push your talk switch and answer me."

Sandra pushed the talk switch forward. "I hear you," she said releasing the switch.

"Don't put your feet on the rudder pedals or hold the joy stick until I tell you."

Sandra again pushed the talk switch. "OK, I won't touch anything."

"Good, here we go!"

Mrs. Kingston looked left and right and yelled, "Clear!" before starting the engine. Once the engine was running, the two soldiers pulled the blocks from under the wheels. Sandra felt the engine vibrations and the wind from the propeller hitting her in the face as the plane slowly began moving out of the hangar and onto the taxiway that lead to the runway.

"Remember what I said about the plane being a tail dragger?" Mrs. Kingston said into the mike. "We have to move back and forth to see what is ahead because of the angle of the cockpit. Don't be worried that we aren't going straight. What do you think so far?"

"The sounds, the wind—it's all so exciting and we haven't taken off yet."

"We will taxi down a little farther and then hold short of the runway. I won't talk to you for a few minutes. You'll hear me talking to the tower and doing the run-up of the engine before taking off, so don't answer me. Just listen until we're in the air."

Sandra watched the other air craft coming and going while the plane moved to the end of the taxiway. When the taxiway ended, the plane stopped and sat idling next to a runway in what was called the run-up area. There the pilot would bring the engine up to full power, check to make sure the engine was running properly and do any last-minute instrument checks before calling the tower. Next to this area was a runway that had big white letters painted on the cement, 27R. Sandra remembered learning about how airplanes flew using the degrees on a compass to navigate. North corresponds to zero degrees, and the angles increase clockwise, so east is 90 degrees, south is 180, and west is 270. Sandra knew they would be taking off on a west heading. The R meant that when there are two parallel runways, one is called right and the other is left so that pilots know which one to use.

Sandra listened as Mrs. Kingston talked to the tower. "Tower this is 75 Hotel requesting permission for takeoff on runway 27 Right."

"75 Hotel, hold for traffic. Will advise when clear."

"Roger, 75 Hotel hold for traffic. Sandra, we'll sit here for a minute until they clear us to take off. It won't be much longer. If you look up and to your right, you'll see a B-17 coming in for a landing. That's the traffic we are waiting for."

Sandra didn't answer and looked to her right. Coming toward the runway was a huge, four-engine plane with a bright landing light heading directly at them. The plane came lower and lower until it flashed by and landed right in front of them. Then it slowed to a stop. Once the bomber had turned off the runway, Sandra heard, "75 Hotel you are cleared for takeoff on runway 27 Right. Maintain heading until out of the traffic pattern. Cleared for training flight over town and then into area 35. Monitor radio frequency 172.5 for traffic."

Sandra felt the engine coming to full power as the plane moved out on the runway and began accelerating. She felt the tail lift off first as the plane gained speed, allowing her to see out the front of the plane as it raced down the runway.

"Sandra, look at the tree at the end of the runway. I think you have an audience."

Sandra looked at the tree and saw what looked like seven large crows flapping their wings. As the plane got closer, she saw what Mrs. Kingston meant by an audience. The gang had come to watch her take off. The boys were waving their arms back and forth as the plane flew low over the tree. Sandra leaned over the edge of the plane and waved back at her friends, suddenly realizing she was flying.

"We're up. What do you think?"

"I was so busy waving at the gang that I didn't even feel us leave the ground. Look how small everything looks."

"I'll fly over your house so you can wave at your mom. Then we'll just fly around a little bit before doing some of the rolls and loops we discussed."

First, they flew over Sandra's house making a sharp ninety degree turn so Sandra could look directly at her house and wave at her mom before flying over the town. After about twenty minutes, Mrs. Kingston said, "We're over area 35 where we are cleared to do some aerobatics. If at any time you feel sick or queasy, tell me right away. If you do get sick, use the bag on your right. Don't be embarrassed—it just happens."

"I feel good. What are you going to do first?"

"First I'll do a roll. I'll drop the nose a little to get some speed, then when you feel me pull the nose up, I'll roll it over and you won't feel a thing. Ready?"

The first roll was so smooth that Sandra asked to do another. After several rolls they did some ninety degree turns and circles and finally a loop. Mrs. Kingston lowered the nose, picking up speed and then pulled the nose up and flew the plane up and over backwards before coming out of the loop and leveling off.

"Sandra, you're doing great! Now are you ready to fly it a little bit? Remember what I taught you. Turn the joy stick right and you go right. Turn it left to go left. Pull back and the plane climbs, and finally push it forward and we go down. Keep your feet off the rubber pedals. I'll do that. Are you ready?"

"OK, tell me when."

"Go ahead and put your hands on the joy stick. I'm letting go now. It's all yours. Keep your hands on the stick and don't talk to me. I'll talk to you and guide you through your first lesson."

Sandra's heart was pounding as she listened to the instructions. First Mrs. Kingston had her turn the stick a little each way so Sandra could see how the plane reacted to small movements of the joy stick. In just a few minutes, Sandra was making slow turns to the right and left, learning how to keep the plane level while turning.

"You're doing great! I'll let you fly us back to the airport before taking over. Just continue to do as I say, and we'll be back at the airport in no time."

The longer Sandra flew, the more relaxed she became, enjoying the clouds, countryside and the incredible sound of the engine and wind as they soared over the landscape. Sandra lost all sense of time until she heard, "You are a natural born pilot. Up on our right is the town and just to the north of that is the Air Force base. When I say let go, do so, and then I'll fly the plane back. Ready? Let go."

Sandra released the joy stick and sat back, enjoying the last few minutes of the flight. Being in the front seat for the landing was so exciting. The nose of the plane was pointed downward. Sandra was amazed how Mrs. Kingston could fly and talk to the tower at the same time. When the plane finally touched down and taxied to the hangar, Sandra pushed the button to talk. "Thanks, Mrs. Kingston! That was the most excitement I've ever had."

"You can now check that off your list!" Mrs. Kingston said bringing the plane to a stop.

Chapter 20

JULY 4TH

Dale sat on the porch swing waiting for Chrissy to come over so they could walk to the park together. While he waited, he thought about the past four weeks of rehearsal leading up to today's 4th of July concert with the Dixieland group. Once school was out, the group met twice a week at East Libertyville Junior High to rehearse with Mr. Jeffrey. They memorized all of the melodies and learned how to improvise to the blues chords. Mr. Jeffrey wanted the group to hear the chord changes and understand what notes and scales went with each chord. For each song, the members wrote out the scales that went with each chord which helped them keep track of where they were. Dale liked the blues scale with its lowered 3rd, 5th, and 7th notes. These notes gave the blues its sad, mournful sound. P.J. called them the "worried" notes.

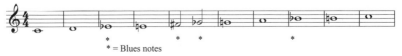

* = Blues notes

They also learned how to bend or scoop notes. Mr. Jeffrey played recordings of jazz artists bending or scooping notes to imitate the original songs or spirituals sung by field hands. Karl had the easiest time since he could use his trombone slide to bend the notes. The other players had to use their lips to lower the pitch and then bring it back up to the correct pitch.

On days where it was too hot to play outside, Chrissy would come over to Dale's house and play the chords of the songs on the piano while Dale improvised. Dale liked improvisation because he could make up the music as he played and it was never the same. Having Chrissy play the piano allowed him to make a lot of mistakes without anyone but Chrissy hearing them. Dale was confident that when his time came to solo at the concert, he would be ready although he was not sure what would come out.

Chrissy called from the sidewalk interrupting Dale's thoughts. He ran down to meet her and they were off to the park.

"How are you feeling about our first performance," Chrissy asked.

"I'm excited and a little nervous about playing jazz for the first time in front of people."

"Don't be. With all of the different acts performing today we'll just be another group to talk over while they eat and celebrate the fourth."

When they got to the town square, all the light poles had red, white, and blue ribbons wrapped around them. The bandstand had buntings hanging on the railings and a big American flag hanging in the back like a curtain. Picnic tables were set out on the grass around the band stand. The streets surrounding the square were closed and there were booths lining the curbs with food, and drink. One entire side of the square had games such as a dunk tank, shooting ducks, and a ring toss.

"Would you look at this place? This is the biggest celebration I've ever seen in Libertyville," Chrissy said as she admired the stuffed animals hanging from the rafters of a booth.

"The whole town is celebrating the victory in Europe. Maybe a big celebration will take everyone's mind off the war in the Pacific. I wish it would end soon, so my dad could come home," Dale said wistfully.

"From what I hear on the radio, the war might be coming to an end very soon," Chrissy said. Then she spotted Victor who was waving his hand for them to join him and the rest of the gang.

"I picked this picnic table by the front of the stage so we could put our cases here while we listen and wait for our turn to perform. What do you think?" Victor said.

"We'll need at least two tables with P.J. bringing his tuba and string bass," Bridget said.

"That's not fair! Mr. Jeffrey said that I should play the *St. Louis Blues* on the tuba like the original and the *Basin Street Blues* on the string bass. It wasn't my idea to bring two giant instruments."

Bridget patted P.J. on the back. "You know I'm just kidding," she said with a smile on her face.

"OK, but sometimes I can't tell the difference."

The group bought some hotdogs and freshly squeezed lemonade at a booth nearby. As they ate, they listened to a variety of local acts. Mr. Baily and his Barber Shop Quartet sang a peppy patriotic medley, followed by Mrs. Vincent, their general music teacher, singing in the Sweet Adeline's, a female version of a barber shop quartet. Mr. Dobbins who ran the diner juggled balls, knives, and bowling pins. He only dropped a couple pins and had to start several times, but he smiled at the crowd, obviously enjoying his own performance. Only two acts were left to perform, seven-year-old Sarah Louise Crabtree, who was dressed as a flag and who would recite the Declaration of Independence and the Libertyville Acting Troupe. While Sarah climbed the steps to the band stand, the group unpacked their instruments and went into the court house to warm-up. The city council that was in charge of the events had a room where the musicians could do warm-ups. They also had ice water for them to drink before going on stage. After some lip slurs and long tones to warm up, Chrissy sat down at the piano and played the tuning note. Once they were tuned, Mr. Jeffrey entered the room.

He gave the group some last-minute instructions. "When we walk on stage, remember to help Dave with his trap set and Chrissy with her piano. This is not as formal as a school concert. We can be more relaxed so help each other get set up."

"Who's going to help me carry my tuba and the string bass?"

"I'll carry the string bass since you play the tuba first. I'll set the string bass in the back for your second number. Now everyone take a piece of Dave's trap set and let's go," Mr. Jeffrey said.

Each member of the group picked up a part of the trap set and walked out to the band stand. The town's theatre group was just finishing as the group arrived.

Mr. Johnson, the mayor, came up and shook Mr. Jeffrey's hand. "The crowd's excited about hearing some jazz. This is the first and only jazz group today. Why don't you go onstage and when you're all set up, I'll introduce you. By the way, what's your group's name?"

They all looked at each other realizing they hadn't selected a name. "Let's make this easy. We're seventh graders and there are seven of us, so how about the E.L.J.H. Seventh Grade Seven," Bobby said. "Agreed?"

"Agreed!" They said in unison moving onto the stage. When they finished setting up and were ready to begin, Bobby said, "You'd better turn around and look at this. You won't believe it."

The group turned to find that the crowd had stopped milling around and had taken seats at the picnic tables or on the grass and were waiting for the group to be introduced.

"Mr. Jeffrey, I thought you said it was not like a school concert," Dale said.

The director smiled and leaned down to look at the group. "I guess I was wrong ... the word is out that you must be good and so they've come to hear you play. Don't worry, they'll love you." He nodded to Mr. Johnson that the group was ready.

"Welcome fellow citizens of Libertyville. We'd like to continue today's entertainment by introducing the East Libertyville Seventh Grade Seven who will perform two Dixieland numbers for you." Mr. Johnson then handed the mic to Dale as the crowd applauded.

"Thanks, everyone! We're going to play two songs for you today. The first one is *St. Louis Blues* by W. C. Handy," Dale said turning back to the group as he put his mute in the bell of his cornet. "Ah one two, ah one two three," he said to start the group. Each player came up to the mic when it was time to solo. First Karl played his solo just like the recording, and when he stepped away from the mic to let Bobby start, he was surprised that the crowd starting clapping. Mr. Jeffrey had warned them that the audience could clap at the end of a jazz solo. But, they didn't expect the enthusiasm with which the crowd responded. Karl smiled widely and bowed to the crowd as Bobby on clarinet stepped forward and took his turn soloing.

In the original recording, the piano went next, but the group opened the solo section so Bridget could play an alto sax solo and Dale could play a cornet solo. When Chrissy's solo ended, the group played the chorus one last time, holding out the last note. Dave then played a drum fill signaling the end of the piece. The crowd applauded wildly, shouting and clapping until Dale stepped to the mic and held up his hand. "Thanks for that warm reception. This is really fun," which was greeted with another round of applause. "Our next number is one you all know, *Basin Street Blues*. We're going to play the famous trombone version featuring our own Karl on trombone. First, I would like to have Mr. Jeffrey stand up because he taught us how to play jazz." Mr. Jeffrey stood up and waved to the crowd.

"Before our final number, we have a surprise for Mr. Jeffrey. Most of the blues songs have words. Now we'd like to bring up one of Libertyville's finest songsters. When we heard his singing for the first time, we thought he sounded just like Jack Teagarden's recording. We worked hard to keep this a secret from Mr. Jeffrey, so here we go. Let's put our hands together for Emerson Grade School's own, Mr. Malone." Mr. Malone came from behind the stage and bowed to the audience.

Stepping to the mic, Mr. Malone said, "Here we go. Ah one, two, ah one two three." The crowd started snapping their fingers and clapping to the beat as his velvety voice captured the hearts of everyone in the audience. At the end of the final verse, he said, "And now a little trombone..." Karl ended the piece with an unaccompanied solo he'd worked on with the group joining him on the last note.

Mr. Jeffrey was the first to stand yelling, "Bravo, Bravo." The crowd that spread out over the entire square gave the group and Mr. Malone a standing ovation.

Dale stepped back up to the mic. "Thanks everyone, but we only know two songs. Next year, be sure to come to one of our jazz concerts at East Libertyville Junior High. We look forward to seeing you then. Thanks again." When the applause died down, Mr. Jeffrey came onto the stage to congratulate his students.

"That was some surprise you pulled today. First you learn a song and sneak in and surprise me before school. And now, today, you surprise me again with a vocal soloist? We need to have an agreement. NO more surprises!" He was grinning from ear-to-ear.

The group laughed and finished putting away their equipment before enjoying all of the games and food before the fireworks at dusk.

"Not only did we play great, but also I got to check off one of the items on my list," P. J. said as he took a bite from a raspberry snow cone. "Come on, I want to shoot the guns at the moving ducks booth."

The gang played several games before entering the area where various groups from the community were having fundraisers. There were home-made baked goods and crafts for sale, as well as a large tent filled with people playing BINGO. The kids watched as each person scanned his card wanting to be the first to call "BINGO."

"Let's go to the VFW dunk tank and see who is getting dunked. I hope it's someone we know," Dale said as the group walked toward the booth. All the money raised by the VFW went to support families of soldiers who were overseas. Dale always enjoyed this booth because people would volunteer to be dunked. Last year Principal Prenty, the mayor, and even Sergeant O'Malley, the police officer, volunteered to get dunked in order to raise money for the soldiers' families.

As they got closer, Dale squinted into the sun. He leaned over to P.J. and said, "Would you look at who's in the tank? It's Jim Petris, that tough kid from the junior high." Dale reached into his pocket and took out a nickel. "I'd gladly pay to get three chances to throw the baseballs and dunk him."

Sitting high on the dunk tank platform, Jim taunted Dale, "Well, if it isn't the big shot cornet player. Looks like you have all your friends to protect you. You even brought some girls with you. I'll bet that's because you throw like a girl."

Sandra turned a bright red and stepped up to the booth. "What do you mean throw like a girl? Are you saying girls can't throw?"

"Yah, I am. Mr. Cornet throws like a girl."

Sandra shook her head in disgust. "There you go with the girl talk again. We'll just have to teach you a lesson. I'll bet you that all three of us girls and Dale can knock you into the water. If we don't, we'll get in the tank, and you can try to dunk each one of us. What do you say to that?"

"That's an easy bet. I'll enjoy dunking all of you. Go ahead take your chances."

"OK, the bet's on. But, you have to stay in the dunk tank until all of us have thrown. Three chances each times four.

That makes twelve possible times that we could knock you in the water. I hope you like getting wet," Sandra said over her shoulder as she paid the money for all of them to play. The man running the booth handed them each three baseballs and showed them where to stand.

"Make sure you stay behind this line when you throw. Hitting the round disk on the arm by the platform will trigger it to collapse and he'll fall into the water. If he falls, he'll have to swim over to the side while we reset the board before he climbs back up. Once he's in the water, wait until we reset the board before you throw again. So far no one has knocked him in. Good luck!"

Sandra walked up to the line, looking at the big red disk about twenty feet away. "I'll go first. No one makes fun of us," she snarled. "Remember, you have to stay in until we're done."

"And, you remember that if I don't get wet, I get a chance to dunk all of you. Take your best shot, Sweetie!" and Jim curled his lip at Sandra.

A crowd began to form as Sandra wound up and released the ball.

"I'm ready when you ..." but before Jim could finish, the ball hit the metal target with a bang, and he was in the water gasping for air.

"I'm sorry, but I couldn't hear what you said," Sandra said mockingly as Jim swam over to the side of the tank. He muttered as he wiped the water from his face and climbed back up on to the board. He glared at her and said, "Beginner's luck," as she released another baseball, once again sending Jim plunging back into the water.

"She must be stepping over the line or something," Jim said to the man who ran the booth as he climbed back on the board for the third time.

"She's not even close," said the vendor, enjoying the crowd that continued to gather. "I think you may have made a bad bet, Sonny."

Sandra didn't even wait for the vender to finish the sentence before she hurled another ball at the disk, hitting it even harder than the last time. When Jim caught his breath and climbed back up on the board, Sandra said, "I guess we cleared up the question if girls could throw or not. Bridget, you're next."

Bridget knocked Jim in the water two out of her three throws, followed by Chrissy who knocked him in once. "That makes six times you've been knocked in the water by us girls. Come on, Dale! Show this kid he should watch his mouth," Sandra said.

Jim just sat on the platform sullenly as he watched Dale step to the line. Dale thought about what his dad had said when he taught him how to pitch. His dad had been a minor league pitcher when he was younger before becoming an engineer for the railroad. "Don't aim, just throw hard. Don't aim, just throw hard." Dale let the ball fly out of his hand just as he said the word "hard" which was followed by a big thunk as the ball smashed into the red disk, sending Jim into the water a seventh time. The group all cheered as Jim slowly swam to the side again.

"I'm sorry, Jim, I forgot to tell you that I was picked for our sand lot team as a pitcher." Before Jim could answer, Dale fired another ball directly into the plate sending Jim in the water.

"This isn't fair," Jim complained to the vendor who ran the booth. "I could drown here."

"Don't whine to me. You made the bet. Now you finish it. OK, last pitch," the vendor said.

The gang shouted and cheered Dale as he stepped to the line one last time. Jim slumped on the platform as Dale raised one finger, signaling the last throw. A loud cheer went up as Jim crashed into the water for the ninth and final time. When he got to the edge of the tank, Sandra walked over and whispered, "I don't think you should say what girls can and can't do," and she turned to her friends with a victory grin. "Let's find something to eat!"

As he climbed out of the tank, Jim glared at the group. "Nobody makes a fool of me!" he muttered, but they were already out of hearing distance.

Chapter 21

PLAN THE PLAN

Three weeks passed since the 4th of July concert. During that time, the Dixieland group had not rehearsed or even talked to Mr. Jeffrey. Everyone needed a break, and the gang spent the time checking off their own firsts, going to movies to escape the scorching July heat, playing at the fort, and swimming in the quarry. Today, however, they would have their final meeting with Mr. Jeffrey to plan the trip to Chicago and Ravinia. As the gang rode their bikes to the junior high, they laughed at how scared they had been the first time they had gone to the junior high for auditions. After eight weeks of rehearsals in the band room, they actually looked forward to going to junior high. The building no longer seemed so large and foreboding.

Dale still had concerns about the bully, Jim Petris, and his friends who always seemed to be around, but he kept those feelings to himself. He couldn't keep Jim's icy stare from the dunk tank out of his mind, and he knew it was inevitable that he would run into him again.

"Hey, Dale! Did you hear me?" Dave said.

"Sorry," Dale said, coming back to reality. "What did you say?"

"I asked you if the girls were meeting us at the junior high."

"I think so ... but if not, we can tell them the details on Sunday when we go over to Chrissy's. It will be fun to listen to the recordings of the music that's going to be played at Ravinia."

"I like the song *Pictures at an Exhibition* the best because of the great tuba parts," P.J. said.

"Me, too! Especially the first movement with the trumpet opening to *The Great Gate of Kiev*," Dale said.

They skidded up to the bike rack at the junior high and ran down the darkened hallway to the band room. P.J. was the first to burst through the door. The girls were already seated.

"About time you arrived," Bridget said, tapping on her watch. "Remember to be early is to be on time, and to be on time is to be late."

"You're right. We didn't race because we were talking about the trip," Bobby said.

Mr. Jeffrey came out of his office. "Either way, I'm glad you're here. Take a packet from the table. I'll talk you through it to make sure you understand where we are going and how you'll have to act. Chicago's a big city and you'll have to stay with me so you don't get lost."

The boys took the packet and had a seat. "If you have any questions, please ask." Mr. Jeffrey stepped up on the podium began reading the itinerary:

Summer of Firsts Trip to Chicago and Ravinia
Saturday, August 11, 1945

6:00 a.m. sharp – Arrive at the train station and board train #1522.

6:30 a.m. – Train departs for Chicago's Union Station. Eat breakfast in the dining car.

10:30 a.m. – Arrive at Union Station.

10:30 a.m. to 4 p.m. – Tour of Chicago: Walk to the Art Institute then enjoy Grant Park and Buckingham Fountain before strolling along Lake Michigan to admire the sky line and watch the naval pilots training at Navy Pier.

4:00 p.m. – Early dinner at the Italian Village, one of the oldest established restaurants in Chicago. You'll need to be on your best behavior and use proper dining etiquette.

6:00 p.m. – Board the Chicago and Milwaukee Electric Railroad North Shore Line at the Merchandise Mart for the train ride to Ravinia. The train will take us directly to the entrance of Ravinia in Highland Park, a suburb of Chicago.

6:30 p.m. – Arrive Ravinia Park for a walking tour of the park.

8:00 p.m. – Seating begins in the pavilion for the concert. Don't forget your tickets!

8:30 p.m. to 10 p.m. – Chicago Symphony Orchestra Concert.

10:30 p.m. – Board the Chicago and Milwaukee Electric back to Chicago.

11:15 p.m. – Arrive Chicago and take a cab to Union Station.

11:45 p.m. – Board train # 2203 for Libertyville.

4:00 a.m. – Arrive back in Libertyville. Please have your family pick you up at the station.

"Does anyone have any questions?"

"We're going to be gone from six o'clock Saturday morning until four o'clock Sunday morning?" Tommy said.

"You'll be able to sleep on the train going up and back, plus you'll be able to relax under the shade of the trees in Ravinia Park before the concert. It'll be a long day but a very exciting and rewarding one."

"What about money. How much should we bring?" Dave said.

"Well, everything but the short train ride to Ravinia and the cab fare back to Union Station is already paid by the brass quintet's Easter Service pay. It wouldn't hurt to have some extra cash, just in case of an emergency."

"Do you have a map we can look at before we go?" Dale said.

Mr. Jeffrey smiled and passed out the maps that were on his stand. "I've marked all the streets we'll walk down and the places we'll visit."

Everyone started talking at once about what it would be like to be in a big city.

"I've never been outside of Libertyville," Bridget said, raising the level of her voice. "Not only are we going to eat in a fancy restaurant, go to a concert, ride a train and see the sights of Chicago, but also I get to do this with my best friends!"

Mr. Jeffrey laughed. "I'm glad you're excited. I've planned everything down to the minute and have made every arrangement possible. It's so well planned you could probably do this by yourselves."

P.J. wiped the sweat from his brow. "Don't say that. I'm not ready to go to a big city by myself."

"Don't worry! I'll be there with you every step of the way." The director then handed out the train and concert tickets and instructed the students to put them in their folder with the maps and itinerary.

"Don't forget, when we meet at the train station in six days," Mr. Jeffrey warned.

As the group walked out to the bike rack, Dale whispered to Victor. "What's the word etiquette mean? I didn't want to say anything in front of the girls and Mr. Jeffrey."

"I'm not sure, but I think it has to do with manners or something," Victor said.

Tommy was the first on his bike. "Let's race to the fire station and pick up the dogs before we go to the Jungle." The gang pedaled furiously in hot pursuit as Tommy led the way.

Chapter 22

ETIQUETTE

Dale sat at the kitchen table sipping his coffee thinking about the upcoming trip to Chicago and Ravinia. He was excited to eat in the dining car on the train and also at the Italian Village. However, he was nervous about what Mr. Jeffrey said about proper etiquette. When grandma sat down for breakfast, Dale decided to ask her what the word meant. She never made him feel dumb when he asked a question.

"Mr. Jeffrey told us we had to use etiquette when we eat during our trip. I talked to Victor, Tommy and P.J. and we don't know what that means."

"Etiquette is just a fancy word for good manners. Remember how when you ask for permission to leave the table, I always want you to say, *May I be excused* instead of *Can I be excused*. Another example is that when you open a door and a person is behind you, you let the other person go in first. Those are examples of manners or etiquette."

"I've never eaten out at a fancy restaurant."

"You probably understand more than you think. I'll tell you what. Why don't you invite your friends over for dinner tonight? I'll set the table like a fancy restaurant and teach you the proper etiquette so you'll feel comfortable when you go to the restaurant in Chicago."

"You'd do that for us? Thanks, grandma!" and Dale gave her a big hug.

She laughed and said, "I might even be able to convince your grandfather to pretend to be a waiter."

Dale was about ready to leave and run out the door before he said, "May I be excused?"

"Yes, you may!"

He put his plate in the sink and was on his bike headed to the Jungle with Scout by his side. The gang was waiting for him at the fort. Dale told them about his grandmother's dinner invitation and how she would teach them proper table manners. They decided that they would stop swimming and playing at three o'clock so they could get cleaned up for the practice dinner at Dale's home. The rest of the day was full of capture the flag and swimming in the quarry.

Victor was the time keeper and reminded the gang that it was time to leave to get ready for the dinner. "I remember my mom telling my dad one time that you should always arrive at least ten minutes early for a dinner party. I think she was trying to teach him some manners. Let's plan on getting to Dale's house at four fifty."

Dale raced home, even though the temperature that afternoon had reached the 90s. He bounded up the stairs and into the living room where he found a small table set with one place setting of dishes. Each dish, glass and piece of silverware had small strips of paper next to it. Then he walked into their dining room where the table was set with eight place settings of china, the kind that grandma only used for special occasions. Grandmother walked in wearing her flowered Sunday dress and put a place card next to the silverware.

"Why do we have two different tables set up?"

"The dining room will be our restaurant. I wanted to duplicate what you'll see when you have a lot of plates and glasses. The single place setting in the living room will be where I demonstrate how to use each item. Once your friends understand the names and purpose of each item, we'll move into the dining room and have a real meal."

Just then grandpa walked in wearing a white shirt and black bow tie with a white towel over his arm.

"How do I look?" he said, turning full circle. "Don't you think I'll make a great waiter?"

Dale nodded. "I'd better hurry and get ready. The gang is going to be here at 4:50 exactly. Victor's mom told his dad, you're never late for a dinner appointment. You're also never more than ten minutes early since sometimes the host is still getting ready."

"It sounds like you've already started to learn dinner etiquette," grandma said as Dale took to the stairs. He put on his dress pants and the shoes that he wore to church. He decided to wear a shirt with a collar since his mom said a collared shirt is proper dinner attire. When he came back downstairs, he said, "I didn't put on a tie, but I will when we go to Chicago."

"You look great! A tie is a bit formal for tonight," grandmother said.

At ten minutes to five, the doorbell rang. P.J. and Victor had arrived simultaneously.

"My, don't you young men look handsome," grandpa said as he opened the door and ushered them in. During the next five minutes, Karl, Bobby, Tommy, and Dave arrived.

Grandma stood next to the little table in the living room. "Let's get started," she said holding up one of the forks. "I'll explain what to do with each item."

"I've never seen so much stuff for one person to use," P.J. said.

"This is not stuff. It is called silverware and dinnerware, and once you understand when and how to use it, it'll not seem so overwhelming. The point of the rules of etiquette is to make you feel comfortable—not uncomfortable." Grandma then proceeded to teach the boys the names of all the items.

Silverware and Dinnerware:

Grandpa came out of the kitchen and interrupted grandma. "If you're ready, I would like to invite you to sit down. I'll begin serving the first course shortly."

"What's a course? I thought we were having dinner." Dave said.

Grandma overheard as she led the boys to the dining room. "We are having dinner, but the word course is used to describe one of several different types of dishes you'll be served." They circled the table and each one stood behind their chair. "Since I'm the only female, one of you young men should pull my chair out for me. You should do the same for Chrissy, Bridget, and Sandra when you're in Chicago."

Victor volunteered to pull out grandma's chair while the other boys started to sit down. "Wait!" grandma instructed. "Men do not sit down until the women are seated. Just remain standing and then you can sit after the girls are seated." Tommy and Dave got back up and waited until Mrs. Rodine sat down. Then they took their seats.

"I'll talk us through the dinner and make corrections as we go. Please ask questions and don't feel badly if I correct you. You only learn by making mistakes."

For the next hour, grandpa played the part of the waiter while the boys learned how to pass food, make conversation and eat correctly. They had to learn to say thank you to grandpa, if he brought them more water, the next course, or removed their dirty plates. They learned not to slurp the soup and how to tip the soup bowl slightly to get the last few spoonfuls. Next, the salad came, which was a wedge of lettuce with blue cheese crumbled on top. Grandma Rodine reminded the boys to use the silverware from the outside in as the main course of roast beef and potatoes was served. Bobby began to cut his entire piece of meat into pieces before eating it, but was stopped by grandmother.

"You should only cut one piece of meat at a time. Don't cut all of your meat at once. Now that you're older, after you cut a piece of meat, you should eat that one before cutting another. This slows you down and helps you to have a conversation while you enjoy your dinner."

As the dinner progressed and the shadows from the sun began to lengthen, the candles in the center of the table produced a soft yellow glow from the flickering flames.

"What do we say when we have to use the restroom?" Tommy said.

"That's a great question. First you would say, *May I please be excused*. Then get up and place your napkin on the left side of your plate. Before you return, wash your hands, and then when seated, return the napkin to your lap. But, let's say one of the girls asks to be excused. One of the men at the table needs to get up and pull her chair out for her. And, when she returns, get up and pull her chair out again as you did for me earlier."

After dessert the boys talked with Grandma Rodine about all the rules just to make sure they understood.

"How do you know when a meal is finished?" Bobby said.

"Well, usually you watch the host. Since you'll be at a restaurant with Mr. Jeffrey, you'll see him pay the waiter and then place his napkin on the table next to him. When he stands, it's a sign that the meal is over."

The grandfather clock in the hall began to chime, ending the conversation. Grandma thanked her attentive guests. "Do you know that we just ate for almost two hours. It seems like we just started. I'm not sure who had more fun, you or me."

Grandpa Rodine came out of the kitchen wiping the sweat from his brow. "I think being a waiter is a lot of work. I'm going to stick to driving trains."

Everyone laughed as Tommy helped grandma with her chair. Each boy shook hands with grandpa and grandma and thanked them for dinner and the etiquette lesson.

After the last boy left, Dale said, "Grandpa, why don't you take Grandma into the living room. I'll get some coffee for you and then do all the dishes while you rest. How does that sound?"

"I didn't teach you that tonight," grandma said softly. "You certainly are growing up to be a polite, young man. Come on grandpa/waiter, let's go sit down. You look like you need a rest."

Chapter 23

NEWS

"I can't believe that it is August tenth already. We only have three weeks of vacation left," Tommy said as he lay back on the cool granite stone of the quarry.

"This summer is going way too fast. I have three more items on my list to finish," Dave said.

Victor sat up. "I hate to change the subject, but did you hear that the Air Force dropped another atomic bomb on Japan yesterday?"

"How'd you hear that?" Dale said.

"I read about it this morning when I was folding newspapers for my paper route."

Dave joined the conversation. "My dad said that we dropped the first atomic bomb on Hiroshima because the Japanese refused to surrender. He mentioned that at some meeting, China, Britain, and the United States had signed a proclamation on July 26 that Japan must immediately agree to surrender unconditionally or face destruction."

"My mom said that the first bomb named *Little Boy* was dropped by a B – 29 named the *Enola Gay* like the one we saw her fly earlier in the summer," Dale said.

"Who would name a bomb *Little Boy*?" Bobby said.

"It's probably the same guy who named the second bomb *Fat Man*," Victor said with authority.

Since Victor seemed so sure of himself, Tommy asked a question he was sure that Victor couldn't answer. "What's the name of the plane that dropped the last bomb?"

"I read that in the paper, too. It was called Boxcar and was a B – 29."

"I feel sorry for the people they bombed. I hope nobody gets angry at our country and drops an atomic bomb on us," Bobby said. "It's kind of scary to think about."

"My dad tried to explain why we did it. He said that if we had to attack the mainland of Japan that the number of soldiers who would die would be massive. Japan is a proud country and would not give up without a fight," Tommy said.

"That's what my grandfather said too," Dale added. "I sure don't want my dad having to go fight on their island."

"All I can say is that this war talk makes me scared. Let's go for one last swim and forget about it. Tomorrow is our big trip to Chicago, and I only want to think of that," Dave said as he jumped on the rope swing and swung out over the water.

One by one, the boys followed Dave by jumping into the cool water.

Chapter 24

CHANGE IN PLANS

It was early and the sky still had a pinkish glow. Dale bounced along in the front seat of the Jeep as his mother drove to the Libertyville train station. He had on his white shirt, dress pants, and his freshly shined shoes. On the floor next to his feet was his pack that had his tie and the folder with his tickets, map, and itinerary. Chrissy was riding with them, and her hair whipped in the wind as they pulled into the station parking lot reserved for military personnel.

Mrs. Kingston turned off the Jeep and said. "Are you both sure that you packed everything?"

Dale glanced at Chrissy. "We both have our tickets, maps, and itinerary. I also have the extra money in my day pack for safe keeping."

"Good! Now remember, although you've been to Chicago several times with your father and grandfather that Mr.

Jeffrey is in charge. It's a big city. Always be aware of your surroundings and never talk to strangers. You must stay together with the group."

Dale and Chrissy promised and each one gave her a hug. Then they went inside the station looking for their friends and train #1522. Although it was early, the station was full of military personnel and families waiting for loved ones. They didn't see any of their friends in the station so they went outside on the platform and read the board that listed what track the trains were on. As Dale stood looking for his train number, he felt a hand on his shoulder. Mr. Paulson, the conductor, was standing next to them.

Dale extended his hand in greeting. "I haven't seen you since my dog Scout and my dad came home in March."

"Has it been that long? Time sure has flown by. I hear you are going to Chicago on the #1522."

"How'd you know that?"

"Your grandfather told me when I saw him the other day. Come along, and I'll show you to your train. I'm the conductor on your train, and I've saved you and your friends some of the best seats."

Dale looked down the track. In the distance, he could see Tommy, Dave, Victor, Bobby, and Karl standing next to the waiting train, jumping up and down waving.

"Mr. Paulson, I'd like to introduce you to my friends if you have time."

"I'd enjoy meeting them, but I have to start loading the passengers. We leave exactly at 6:30," he said, taking his pocket watch out to check the time.

Dale and Chrissy hurried down the platform to meet their friends. He pointed at the conductor and explained excitedly that Mr. Paulson had saved them some seats.

Before he got on the train, the conductor came up and introduced himself to the group. "When Mr. Jeffrey gets here and you get on the train, come to car number three. I'll be waiting for you."

"That's really nice of you," Victor said shaking his hand.

As Mr. Paulson got on the train, Chrissy looked frantically around. "Where's the rest of our group? I don't see Bridget, Sandra, P.J., or Mr. Jeffrey." She glanced at her watch. "Mr. Jeffrey is never late!"

Dale reassured her. "I'm sure he's just taking care of some last-minute details. Here come Bridget and Sandra as we speak." The three girls hugged each other as if they hadn't seen one another in years.

Moments later, they watched as P.J. ran down the platform toward them with his shirt hanging out and sweat running down his face. "Sorry, I'm late, but I went to the wrong track," he said as he tried to catch his breath. "When the conductor told me I was getting on the wrong train, I ran as fast as I could so I wouldn't miss it." He took out a handkerchief and wiped off his face. "Hey, where is Mr. Jeffrey?"

"I don't know, but he'd better hurry. My watch says the train leaves in ten minutes," Victor said.

From a loudspeaker above the platform, a loud voice boomed, "All aboard, all aboard the #1522 to Chicago."

Bridget looked at each of her friends' faces. "What should we do? They're calling our train and Mr. Jeffrey isn't here."

Dale decided to take charge. "Why don't you board the train and go to the third car where Mr. Paulson is waiting. I'll wait here until Mr. Jeffrey arrives. Don't worry. He'll be here soon, and I'll show him where we're sitting."

"Are you sure? What if..." Dale cut Sandra off and said, "It'll be fine. Just get on, and we'll meet you." Karl was the first to climb the three steps into the train car while Dale paced back and forth waiting for their director.

The platform emptied as the people going to Chicago boarded. Finally, the conductor who was standing next to Dale said, "Last call, last call! All aboard." Dale worriedly looked in both directions, but there was no one in sight.

"Son, either you get on the train or we'll leave without you." A loud hiss of the steam escaping from the brakes startled Dale. He knew the train was about to leave. *Maybe Mr. Jeffrey got on the train through another door*, he thought. Dale climbed the stairs to the train and took one final look down the platform, but Mr. Jeffrey was not in sight. He made his way down to car number three as the train jerked to a start, nearly throwing him into the lap of a service man who was reading a paper. *Mr. Jeffrey's probably sitting with the gang in car number three already.*

Dale took a deep breath as he opened the door to car three and made his way down the aisle to where his friends sat. Mr. Paulson had saved four sets of two seats that faced each other on both sides of the car so they were together. Searching the faces of the passengers, he realized that Mr. Jeffrey wasn't one of them.

Victor was the first to spot Dale approaching. He pointed and the others turned around to see the boy walking toward them by himself. He watched as his friends displayed a variety of expressions. Bridget had her hand over her mouth, P.J. looked bewildered, Victor frowned, and Dave's lips tightened. Dale looked at his friends and stood in silence.

Finally Tommy said, "Where's Mr. Jeffrey? He's coming, isn't he? He did make the train?"

Dale shook his head. "I don't think so, unless he got on the train and I didn't see him."

"So you think he missed the train?" Chrissy said in a worried voice.

"I think we're on our own," Dale finally admitted. "Don't worry! At least we have Mr. Paulson to ask for help."

Dale slid into the seat next to Sandra. He decided to remain positive and explained to the gang that he'd been to Union Station before and that he had money so they could call home after they arrived. His face brightened, "We're safe on the train and we have a reservation in the dining car for breakfast. Let's eat and then rest before the adventure begins."

Tommy agreed. "At least we're together. If we work as a group, we can make this exciting. After all, we *are in seventh grade!*"

Chrissy, however, expressed concern. "This just doesn't seem like Mr. Jeffrey. You don't think something bad happened to him, do you?"

Before anyone could answer, Mr. Paulson had come down the aisle to take their tickets. "Welcome aboard! I'll need your tickets," he said and he punched the tickets before returning them. "By the way, where is Mr. Jeffrey?"

"We don't have any idea. I'm not sure what we should do," Dale said handing his ticket to Mr. Paulson.

"Don't worry. This train is going straight to Chicago. When we get there, I'll show you where the phones are, and you can call your folks. For now, I'll show you the dining car. You can relax and enjoy the ride."

P.J.'s good humor returned and he stood up. "I'm hungry. Food always helps me think."

They followed the conductor as he led them through several cars toward the back of the train. The last door opened into a brightly lit car filled with tables with white tablecloths on both sides of the aisle.

A man in a white coat introduced himself. "I'm Mr. Simmons, and you must be the group from East Libertyville

Junior High. We have a reserved table right here," and he gestured for them to sit down.

Dale, sensing that the girls were nervous, pulled out a chair for Chrissy as he had been taught by his grandmother. The other boys followed Dale's lead.

"Thanks, Dale," Chrissy said shyly.

"Thanks, Victor," Bridget said

"Thanks, Tommy," Sandra purred.

Once the girls were seated, the boys took their seats and put their napkins in their laps.

Bridget noticed and was impressed. "How'd you all get so polite?"

Dale winked at Victor. "Are you saying we haven't always been that way?"

Mr. Simmons poured each person a glass of water and handed them a menu. "Our chef told me that he would be right out to talk to you. I don't know who you are, but you must be very special. He never comes out to greet passengers."

"You don't think we're in trouble, do you?" Dave said.

"How can we be in trouble if we just got here," Karl said smiling and examining the menu.

"Don't worry. I'm sure it's nothing." Dale stopped in mid-sentence when he saw a man in an all-white outfit with a chef's hat on working his way toward the table. Dale stood and hugged him to the surprise of his friends.

"Mr. Edwards! When did you get back from the war? I haven't seen you in almost three years." The large man put his hands on Dale's shoulders as he looked him up and down.

"I got back about a month ago, and they gave me back my chef's job on the train. I heard you were coming today and had to say hello. Who are all these fine looking young people with you?"

Dale introduced his friends who all stood and shook Mr. Edwards's hand.

"My pleasure! I've been a friend of the Rodines and Kingstons, two of the greatest railroad families, for over twenty years. I've known Dale since he was in diapers." The group laughed for the first time that day, and Dale's faced flushed with embarrassment. "How's your dad doing?"

"He's still in the Pacific," giving Mr. Edwards a worried look. "We get letters every so often, but he can't tell us where he is."

"He's a good man and a great train engineer. If I can survive the war, then so can he. I'm going to cook you one fine breakfast. And by the way, I talked to a friend of mine, Mr. Malone."

"You mean the one from the Emerson School?" P.J. said.

"The one and only! He told me that you played some blues at the 4th of July celebration."

"That's right, we formed a Dixieland combo and played *Basin Street Blues* and *St. Louis Blues*. Do you know those songs?"

"Do I know them?" and Mr. Edwards laughed deeply. "I've heard them played live by both Louis Armstrong and Jack Teagarden in Chicago. When you get back to Libertyville, give me a call, and I'll let you listen to some of my recordings."

After the chef returned to the kitchen, Bridget leaned forward and said, "Do you know everybody on this train?"

"No, but they do know my grandfather and my father," Dale said proudly.

Chrissy sat back and gazed out the window. "I'm feeling a lot better now. After breakfast, let's plan our next move once we get to Union Station."

Chapter 25

SELLING THE PLAN

Bridget pressed her face against the window after they returned to their seats. "Look at all the tall buildings! I've never seen anything like it in my life!"

The four-hour ride had passed quickly. The breakfast prepared for them by Mr. Edwards consisted of sausage, freshly squeezed orange juice, pancakes, and omelets oozing with cheddar cheese. Dave and Victor even had their first cups of coffee after seeing Dale order a cup with cream. After breakfast, they planned what to do once they got to Chicago. They studied the itinerary and the maps and discussed the options of either waiting in Union Station until it was time to take the return train home to Libertyville or go ahead with the original trip. Everyone shared feelings for or against, but Dale saved his opinion for last.

"No matter what we decide, we've gotten to know each other better and are closer friends than ever. I suggested this trip as a group activity for our lists, but I had no idea that it would be such an exciting adventure. I don't want it to end."

Dale looked out the window as the train passed the narrow buildings and factories that lined the tracks.

"I've been to Chicago three times and Mr. Jeffrey has given us the addresses of the restaurants, train stations, and Ravinia. We have maps and the tickets. Everything is paid for except the cab from the Merchandise Mart to Union Station. We've got money, and it's going to be daylight most of the time. Victor has a watch. Tommy, Karl, and Dave are the best map readers I've ever seen." Tommy nodded his head in agreement.

"We're smart and we can figure this out. Let's call home when we get off the train, because now we're going to have to convince our parents to let us go ahead with the trip."

Chrissy jumped into the discussion. "I hope we can find out what happened to Mr. Jeffrey. I'm sure he didn't do this to us on purpose!"

They all agreed, and then Dale said, "To do this right we should take a vote. To make it fair, close your eyes so no one can see how each person votes. I'll ask Mr. Paulson who's coming down the aisle to count the number of hands raised if you want to continue the trip. If the vote for yes is five or more, then we'll try to convince our parents. Agreed?"

"Agreed!" they all said.

Mr. Paulson approached their seats. "Won't be much longer until we get to the station. Hope you had a good time."

"We're going to take a vote on what to do next. Would you count the votes? We'll close our eyes. When you're done counting, tell us to put our hands down," Dale said.

"We'll need to hurry. We're getting close to the station."

"OK, I'll count to three and then raise your right hand if you want to continue the trip. One, two, three...vote."

After a moment of silence, Mr. Paulson said, "Lower your hands and open your eyes. That was easy—it was unanimous."

"What does that mean?" P.J. said.

"Sorry, I mean everyone voted yes. Now I'll want to hear how you'll convince your parents to continue your trip on your own. Once we stop, stay put while the other passengers depart. I'll come back and walk you to the phones," and with that he left to prepare for the arrival at Union Station.

Dale turned to his friends. "Thanks for wanting to continue the trip. Now let's talk about how to explain our plan to our parents."

They discussed various ways and decided to let Dale be the first to talk.

"OK, but I want all of you to listen. I may need you to get on the phone one at a time to talk."

Sandra agreed. "You should let Bridget, Chrissy, and me talk. If our parents hear that we're comfortable with the plan, I think they'll let us stay."

"You can't let them hear any doubt or fear in your voice when I hand you the phone," Dale warned.

The three girls put their hands together in a pact. "We won't let you down."

The train slowed to a crawl as it pulled into the station. Even though it was daylight, it was very dark. Steam hissed from the brakes as the train slowed to a stop. The air was filled with fumes from trains idling on the tracks that ran parallel to their train. The passengers stood and lined up in the aisle in preparation for departure. The doors opened, and the people streamed out and onto the platform.

After the cars emptied, just as he had promised, Mr. Paulson returned. "Time to go. I'll take you to the west side of the station to the waiting room we call the Great Hall. You can call home from there. I overheard some people talking about news that the war could possibly end very soon."

They followed Mr. Paulson down the aisle, and the boys helped the girls down the steep train steps onto the platform. As they walked through the crowd, P.J. yelled, "Oh, no! I left my pack with my tickets on the train!" Before anyone could say anything, he bolted back to the train and disappeared into the car. In a few minutes, he emerged victorious with his pack in his hand and a smile on his face.

They continued the walk to the station. They huddled next to one another as a train on the next track edged next to them, its brakes grinding the cars to a halt. They gazed up at the tall engine and the engineer waved down to them. Crowds of people loaded with luggage surged past them as they stayed close to Mr. Paulson.

They entered the station, which had a high, vaulted ceiling held up by tall columns. Their shoes echoed on the polished marble floors. Rows of long wooden benches were filled with people as if they were waiting for a church service to begin. A baby cried inconsolably as its mother tried to comfort it.

On the far side of the waiting room was a row of phones. People were talking animatedly.

"I've never seen so many people or such a huge room," Karl said looking up at the sunlight streaming in through the skylights overhead.

"Stay together," Victor urged, and he hurried to catch up with Mr. Paulson.

Mr. Paulson stopped abruptly at an open phone. "Make your call. And, when you are done, wait on this bench until I come back. We can discuss what your parents want you to do. I won't be long."

They gathered around Dale who went to the phone farthest away from all of the other people. He took a deep breath and said, "Here we go."

Picking up the phone Dale waited for the operator to come on the line. "Yes, operator, I'd like to make a collect call to Libertyville, Indiana, to C. H. Rodine, number 5-0126." Dale put his hand over the receiver. "The operator is connecting me. It won't be long."

The chatter of conversation in the waiting room was so loud that Dale had to put a finger in one ear. "Thank you, operator."

"Yes, we're fine." Dale nodded his head to the group.

"We're all together in Union Station. Mr. Paulson brought us here and is looking after us."

"What? Can you speak louder?"

"You said Mr. Jeffrey is with you? What happened to him? We were worried."

Dale furrowed his brow. "You say he had an accident?"

Dale motioned to the group to come over to him. "He hit a deer and crashed in the ditch outside of town this morning. Is he OK?" Dale nodded his head to let his friends know that Mr. Jeffrey was alright.

"I understand you were worried, but we're fine."

"Everyone's parents are at our house?"

"We're fine. Can you please tell them that?"

Dale put his hand over the receiver and spoke to the group while his mom talked to the other parents. "I'm going to tell them our plan," he said.

"We understand that you're concerned, but we took a vote, and we want to go ahead with the trip."

Dale kept nodding and saying "yes" while the group watched his every word.

Finally, P.J. couldn't stand it any longer. "What are they saying?" he yelled.

Dale ignored him and kept talking. "But, we have everything we need. I've been to Chicago three times. We have maps, tickets, and everything has been paid for," and Dale continued spouting off all of the reasons why they should be allowed to continue the trip as planned.

Dale covered the receiver with his hand. "My mom's talking to your parents. I hear a lot of discussion in the background. I'm not sure how it's going." Then he continued the conversation with his mom.

"I understand we're only twelve, but everything is planned and we're here anyway. We can't catch the next train to Libertyville until this evening anyway."

Dale pleaded.

He motioned to Bridget. "Your mom wants to talk to you. Here," and he handed the phone to her.

She took a deep breath and spoke calmly. "Yes, we're fine," and she turned and lowered her voice. "You know I wouldn't ask to stay if I were scared. I'd never do anything that wasn't planned and organized."

Bridget listened and tapped her foot impatiently. Then she said emphatically, "Yes, all of the girls want to stay."

"OK, I will. I love you."

One by one, each one got on the phone and reassured their parents that they were fine and they wanted to stay. Dave, who was last, handed the phone back to Dale.

"Hi, Mr. Jeffrey, are you alright?"

"I'm glad that you only have some stitches and bruises."

"I understand you're sorry, but you have to help us out. We can really do this trip on our own. You know we have everything we need. Can you convince our parents?"

Dale listened while Mr. Jeffrey talked. Then he put his hand over the receiver. "Mr. Jeffrey is going to suggest to our parents that he call his contacts at the Italian Village restaurant and Ravinia. He also has a friend that could drive us to Union Station after the concert. He thinks that if he has someone meet us at each place, the parents might agree to let us stay. It's a long shot, but it's worth a chance." Dale pressed the phone to his ear. "I can hear a lot of discussion going on in the background."

Then he said, "I'm still here."

"How will I know who they are?"

"Wait...I have an idea. Let's have a password like they do in the war movies."

"How about Oskee Wow Wow? You remember from the University of Illinois fight song?" Dale's voice quickened with excitement.

"I'll say the first part Oskee, and they'll have to answer Wow Wow. If they don't say that, then we'll know they are strangers and not to go with them."

Dale waited while the adults on the other end of the line debated.

Karl tapped Dale on the shoulder. "What do you think? Are they going to let us stay?"

"SHHHH...they're coming back on."

Dale listened intently and smiled. "I promise that we'll call if anything goes wrong."

Then he looked at Mr. Paulson who had been standing behind the group listening. "My mom wants to talk to you."

Mr. Paulson moved through the group to get to the phone.

"Hello, I'm fine and so are the children."

"They are very grown up for their ages, and so far, they have handled themselves splendidly."

Then he thought of one more thing to say, "And, just so you feel better, I'm the conductor on the return train tonight. I'll make sure they are well taken care of."

Mr. Paulson hung up and turned to find ten pairs of eyes glued on him. "Your parents have decided to let you stay. I'm to escort you to Jackson Street and show you where you are on your maps. They reminded me to tell you to stay together. I'll be here to meet you at the station after the Ravinia concert. What's that you're supposed to say?" and he scratched his head as if in thought.

"Oskee!" they yelled, startling the man at the next phone booth.

"Wow Wow!" Mr. Paulson said in return. "Now follow me."

Chapter 26

Execute the Plan

Following Mr. Paulson through Union Station was not easy. The group of ten threaded their way through the throngs of passengers hurrying to catch their trains or saying their last goodbyes. Everyone they passed seemed to be talking very animatedly and the excitement in the air was tangible.

"Mr. Paulson, are people always so loud in Chicago?" Bridget said.

"Take a look at the newsstands. Do you see the headlines?" he said as he kept walking. "The front pages are full of reports about the war. After the bombing of Hiroshima and Nagasaki last week, we may see an end to the war within the next few days. If that happens, what a celebration there will be!"

They came to a large stairway leading out of the cavernous station. They exited through tall glass and metal doors into the brilliant sunlight. As their eyes adjusted, they heard the sounds of a big city: car horns honking; taxicab doors slamming; people's heels clicking on the pavement; train whistles blowing; and everywhere people talking.

Circled around Mr. Paulson, the group stared up at the buildings. Sandra was the first to speak. "I have never seen so many people and large buildings. I thought it would be exciting, but nothing as exciting as this."

A man with a leather briefcase bumped P.J. as he hurried to catch a cab.

Mr. Paulson moved the group over to the edge of the sidewalk. "Please pay attention, and get out your maps. This street is Jackson and if you go east," he said pointing down the street, "you'll run into Lake Michigan. The city is divided into east and west. You must stay on the streets that say east. Right now you are on the corner of Jackson and Canal."

"I see where we are," Tommy said proudly. "I've studied this map for hours. The streets that run east and west are all named after presidents: Adams, Monroe, and Washington, for example. Every block is one-eighth of a mile. That means eight blocks equal one mile. If we count the blocks, we'll have an idea of how far we have to go and how long it'll take to get to the next location."

"I told you he's the best map reader around," Dale said.

"Remember, stay together. I'll meet you back here at Union Station at eleven p.m. sharp. Trains don't wait for passengers, so don't be late." They all thanked Mr. Paulson and promised to be back at the station on time.

The group crossed the bridge over the Chicago River with Tommy and Dale, the official map readers leading the way, followed by the boys on the outside and the girls on the inside. Although the streets were crowded, they became more confident about navigating through the throngs of people. Victor became the official tour guide pointing out famous buildings and landmarks along the way. P.J. became the unofficial traffic patrol guide and made sure the light had changed and the traffic was clear at each intersection before signaling it was OK to cross. Bobby, Dave, and Karl walked on the outside of the group, making sure everyone was together.

"I estimate we've gone about a mile. We should be able to see Lake Michigan and Grant Park in another block," Tommy said.

"Before we go to the park, I want to stop at the Art Institute and see the two lion statues that are in the front," Victor said.

"I've got a surprise for everyone," Chrissy said as she pulled a camera from her big purse. "I talked my dad into giving me his camera and two rolls of film. I think our first group picture should be in front of the lions. If we take group pictures at each place we go, I'll get them developed and make a scrapbook for everyone. I want to remember this day forever."

Tommy pointed across Michigan Avenue. "Here's your first photo opportunity."

"Let's not get too excited until we've crossed the street," P.J. said pushing his way to the curb and holding his arms out to block the path.

They heard a deep laugh behind them. "It looks like we have a policeman in the making," the voice said. "What's your name, young man?"

P.J. turned to face a policeman in a blue uniform with a large badge and night stick. "P.J. Walsh, officer."

"You've got a fine Irish name. I'm officer O'Brien, and I've been following you kids for the last several blocks. Do you have a chaperone or an adult with you?"

Dale stepped forward. "Our chaperone missed the train we were on, and we convinced our parents to let us continue the trip alone."

Dale then handed the officer a map and itinerary. "Hmmm. You seem to be organized from what I see. You have maps and specific times and places to go to." He handed the map and itinerary back to Dale. "Just remember, this is a big city and you must always be aware of your surroundings. I'll help you across Michigan Avenue, and I'll be glad to take your first group picture by the lions."

The officer stepped into the street, holding his arms out for the traffic to stop.

After crossing the four lanes, Victor raced P.J. to the foot of the bronze lion that stood regally guarding the entrance to the museum. Chrissy handed the camera to the officer and arranged her friends around the statue. She had Sandra and Bridget sit on the front paws with her in the center. The boys filled in around them. She waved to the officer that they were ready.

"I don't think I have to ask you to smile," he said as he took the shot.

As the policeman handed Chrissy the camera, she said, "Wait! Can we take a picture of you pretending to arrest us? It'll be a joke we can pull on our parents."

The officer smiled. "Sure, I like a good joke." He waved over another officer to take the picture. As they stood under the lion, Officer O'Brien held Dale by the arm as he pointed his baton at Tommy and Dave as if telling them they were under arrest."

They shook hands with the officers, and raced up the steps to the museum. After a short stay, they continued their sight-seeing expedition. They took group pictures in front of Buckingham Fountain, the Natural History Museum, and the Shedd Aquarium. They posed on the steps of Soldier Field, where the Chicago Bears play football. They even bought a hot dog from a street vendor.

Dave said, "That was the finest hot dog I've ever had. Now I can check *Eat something from a food cart* off my list."

"That makes two of us," P.J. said wiping the mustard off his face.

The final photo of the afternoon was a picture standing in the waters of Lake Michigan. The boys took off their shoes and socks, rolled up their pants and waded out into the water. The girls, not wanting to get wet, climbed on the backs of Victor, Dale, and Tommy. Chrissy asked a passing sailor to take the picture. She said that anyone in uniform could be trusted with her camera. When the picture was finished, they sat on the rocks in the warm sun, letting their feet dry and planned the next part of their trip.

"We have about a mile to walk to the Italian Village for dinner. We have an hour so that'll give us plenty of time," Tommy said

P.J. jumped up. "Let's get going. I'm starved from all this walking."

"When aren't you hungry? You just had a hot dog an hour ago," Bobby said.

The group walked back through Jackson Park and crossed Michigan Avenue back into the downtown area.

Tommy held up his map and pointed. "One more block and we're there."

Sandra stopped and took off her shoe, examining a large blister that was starting to form. "My feet are killing me."

"I see it!" Dave said pointing down the street at a building with three large rounded glass doors. There was a large canopy with three shields announcing the Italian Village over the entrance of the restaurant.

Before they entered, they huddled outside. Dale said, "When we go inside, let me do the talking. I'll use the password when we get inside."

The boys held the doors for the girls just as Grandma Rodine had instructed. In contrast to the outside, the foyer of the restaurant was dark.

Dale stepped forward to give the password to a man at the front entrance, but before he could say anything, a short, lively woman came bursting through the kitchen doors. She ran up to Dale and took his hand in hers. "Finally! I've been thinking about you all day," she said giving him a hug. Dale stood there and glanced at his friends, not knowing what to do. The woman put her arm around him and turned him toward the man at the desk who was smiling broadly. "I'm Ada Capitanini and this is my husband Alfredo. When Mr. Jeffrey called me this morning and told me you were touring the city by yourselves, I was worried sick." Mrs. Capitanini hugged each member of the group before her husband said, "Follow me, we have a table waiting for you."

They followed the Capitaninis into the dining room that had dark, polished wooden walls filled with tables covered with white linen. With a flourish, Mr. Capitanini waved his arm toward a large round table in the center with twelve place settings. Mrs. Capitanini shooed the group toward the table. "Sit, sit, you must be starved. I hope you don't mind if Alfredo and I join you for dinner. We want to hear all about your trip."

P.J. pulled out a chair for his hostess, "Mrs. Capitanini, may I seat you."

"My, what a polite young man! Will you sit next to me?"

P.J. blushed as he waited for the girls to be seated.

Once they were all seated, Dave nudged Dale. "This table looks just like your grandma's table. I'm not nervous at all about which fork to use or anything."

The Capitaninis laughed. Mr. Capitanini said, "I hope you don't mind, but we've already ordered dinner for you," and for the next hour and a half, waiters hovered over them, bringing fresh Italian bread, antipasto, spaghetti and meatballs, and lasagna.

During the dinner, the conversation flowed. Dale said, "How'd you get to know Mr. Jeffrey?"

"We first met him when he was a university student. He'd come to take lessons and hear the symphony, and afterwards, he'd always come to the restaurant. He loved our fettuccini Alfredo," and Mr. Capitanini winked. "It's not really named after me, but I like for my customers to think so."

Mrs. Capitanini interrupted her husband. "Many of our customers are music lovers who either play in the Lyric Opera or the Chicago Symphony. I love music, and I must admit that if I hadn't met Mr. Capitanini, I'd have been an opera singer," she said as her husband patted her hand.

Just then the waiters brought a large silver platter of cannoli for dessert. P.J. had to loosen his belt a notch. After dessert, the girls excused themselves to freshen up. The boys all stood when the girls stood, and when they returned, the boys pulled out their chairs to seat them.

At the end of the meal, the Capitaninis stood. "It's been our pleasure to have a dinner with such well-mannered, and might I say, good-looking young men and women. If the rest of the young people in this country are like you, then we have a bright future," Mr. Capitanini said. At that moment, a man in a suit walked over to the table and waited patiently until the host was finished.

"Sir, I have the car outside, so your guests don't miss their train to Ravinia."

"Thank you, Anthony. Please take good care of our guests so that they get to the station on time."

Everyone hugged Mrs. Capitanini and shook Mr. Capitanini's hand. "Thanks for the dinner. I don't think I'll ever be hungry again," P. J. said as he patted his stomach.

Mrs. Capitanini motioned to a waiter. "I've packed a little food in case you get hungry before the concert. At Ravinia, you can sit on the grass under the trees before the concert and have a picnic," she said as the waiter set a large basket covered with a red-checked napkin. She said wistfully, "I wish I were going," as they walked to the entrance of the restaurant.

Mrs. Capitanini grabbed Dale's hand. "Remember, you're part of our family now. You be sure to come back and see us when you come back to Chicago," she said as she walked them outside.

On the sidewalk in front of the restaurant, Chrissy asked Anthony to take a picture of everyone with the Capitaninis. Then they piled into a large, black Buick sedan. Tommy, the navigator, sat in the front seat with Dale and Anthony as they wove through the congested streets of Chicago.

When they pulled up to the station, Anthony said, "After the concert, you'll take the train and get off at this station. It's called the Chicago Merchandise Mart. Then you'll catch a cab back to Union Station. Buy your round-trip tickets at the window right up those stairs," he said as he hopped out of the car and opened the trunk. "Good luck and here's the food Mrs. Capitanini packed for you."

They bounded up the stairs for the next leg of their Chicago adventure.

Chapter 27

RAVINIA

As they sat on the benches waiting for the train, Tommy said, "So far, we've done a great job navigating our way around the city and not getting lost."

Dale agreed. "And, from here on, we're either on a train or at a concert. The hardest part is behind us."

At exactly six o'clock the train pulled into the station, and the crowd carrying blankets and picnic baskets began loading. The cars were so crowded that they stood and held on to the poles or the straps so the adults could sit. The cool air conditioning felt good after being on the hot sidewalks of the city all day. The only other time they had been in air conditioning was at the movie theater.

The conductor came through the car and punched a hole in the ticket next to their stop, Ravinia. They listened carefully as the conductor announced the name of each stop along the way.

"I'm glad he calls out the name of the station. I wouldn't know which one was the Ravinia stop," Sandra said.

"I'd bet you'd know," Dale said pointing out the window. She could see two large stone pillars with an arched sign with the word Ravinia stretching between them.

Everyone laughed as the conductor said. "Ravinia, Ravinia station next."

When the train slowed to a stop, they followed the crowd as it streamed into the entrance of the park. They stood under the Ravinia sign.

"What do we do now?" Bobby said as the crowd moved toward the gate. Before anyone could answer, a woman approached, standing directly in front of them with her hands on her hips.

Dale stepped forward and said, "Oskee?"

The women broke into a huge smile and responded, "Wow Wow. Mr. Jeffrey asked me to meet you. My name is Roberta Simpson, and I'll be your escort at Ravinia."

"Nice to meet you," Dale said and he introduced each member of the group.

"Let me give you a short tour of the park and tell you some of the history before the concert begins. Please take your tickets out and follow me." They walked past the main entrance, and Mrs. Simpson said, "Back in 1904, Ravinia was an amusement park complete with a baseball diamond, rides, a casino building, and dining rooms. The theatre on your right is the only building on the grounds that dates back to that original construction. The first piece to be heard on the Ravinia grounds, *Bill Baily, Won't You Please Come Home,* was played on a steam calliope."

"I've heard a calliope at the circus once. They're really loud," Dave said.

"Then in 1936, the Chicago Symphony began to use the park as its summer home. You'll hear them tonight."

"They only play here in the summer?" Karl asked.

Mrs. Simpson nodded. "The rest of the time they perform at Orchestra Hall in Chicago."

"That's one of the buildings where we had our pictures taken today. I can't wait to hear the orchestra," Victor said.

"It sounds like you had a chance to tour the Windy City today."

"No," Dave said, "we toured Chicago."

Mrs. Simpson smiled. "Chicago is also called the Windy City because the wind off the lake blows all the time."

P.J. laughed. "Hey, Chicago has a nickname just like I do."

"If you don't be quiet, we'll call you Windy P.J." Chrissy said kiddingly.

Everyone laughed as the tour continued. Mrs. Simpson pointed to a large quilt spread on the ground with a small table of drinks next to it. "Since Ravinia is a park, people come to eat and listen to the concert on the lawn or sit on the seats in the open air pavilion. Before you take your seats in the pavilion, I thought you might enjoy sitting here until the concert starts. Enjoy some lemonade, and I understand you brought some food as well."

"How did you know we have food?" Victor said.

"Don't think that Mrs. Capitanini isn't keeping track of you. She's a great patron of the arts who makes sure that her special guests are taken care of. Now relax and enjoy the time before the concert starts. I'll meet you at the back of the pavilion after the concert to escort you to the train," and Mrs. Simpson left while they spread out on the blanket.

"I feel very important that I'm a special guest," Bridget said.

Chrissy sat down next to her. "I can't believe how beautiful this place is. Can you imagine what it's like to lay here under the stars and listen to music? It can't get better than that."

"Especially when you're with your best friends," Karl said.

"Stop, you're going to make me cry," Sandra said gently punching him in the shoulder.

"He's right! It's been a great trip so far, but we still have a concert and two train rides to go. I don't think the fun is over yet," Dale said as he paged through the program.

P.J. handed everyone a drink, and then he opened the basket of food.

They studied their programs and munched on the sausage, cheese, olives, and more cannoli that Mrs. Capitanini had packed.

In preparation for the concert, Mr. Jeffrey had explained the history concerning each piece and composer. He preached that knowing the background of the music would make the concert more enjoyable. During their summer meetings at the junior high band room, they listened to recordings of the pieces. He also let the group take the records home so they could listen on their own.

"I've got an idea," Sandra said. "Let's play a game where we quiz one another about the music and anything we've learned about the pieces being played tonight. We can use the notes in the program to create questions. The one with the most points wins," Sandra said.

"But what do we win?" Dave said.

After a short discussion, it was decided that the winner would get first pick of the seats in the pavilion. The loser had to buy ice cream for everyone at intermission. To select the order they would ask questions, they played "Paper, Rock, Scissors." Karl won and Bridget was appointed the score keeper since she always had paper and pencils with her.

"The first question is for Tommy. What does the word overture mean in the title of the first piece, *Overture to Russlan and Ludmilla?*"

Tommy thought for a moment. "I think an overture is a piece that comes before an opera. It's where all of the important songs are highlighted. It's kind of like a preview for a movie. You see a few scenes from the next movie that makes you want to go see it."

"That's correct," Bridget said. "Dale, you ask the next question."

"This question is for Sandra. What do the numbers in the second song, Symphony No. 6, Opus 53, by Shostakovich mean?"

Sandra frowned and insisted that was really two questions.

"If you get them both right, you'll get two points."

"The first number, six, is the number of symphonies Shostakovich wrote. Opus 53 means that this symphony is his fifty-third piece of music that he's written?"

"How can anybody write so much music?" Bobby said.

"I don't know, but she's right. Two points. Dave, you're next," Bridget said.

"This question is for P.J. What do all of the composers in tonight's concert have in common: Glinka, Shostakovich, Tchaikovsky and Mussorgsky."

P.J. rubbed his chin. "First they are all males."

Bridget wasn't amused. "I mean more than just that."

"I'm still right. If I get another thing they have in common right, I get another point. Sandra got two, so why not me?"

"I guess to be fair you should get two points."

"That's easy. They're all Russian composers." P.J. jumped up and squatted down and imitated a Russian Cossack dancing, almost upsetting all the drinks.

"Quit drawing attention to us," Bridget said hastily. She tallied up the score. "I say you not only get the second point for your answer, but your dance earned you an extra point for a total of three."

The game continued with questions ranging from definitions of *largo, allegro,* and *presto* to how many players were in a string quartet, which Victor answered correctly.

"No fair," P.J. complained. "That's like asking him who's buried in Grant's tomb."

Finally the score was tied between Bridget and P.J. Dale got to ask the last question. Dale thought for a moment before he said, "What was the name of the painter who painted the pictures that the last piece, *Pictures at an Exhibition,* is based upon."

Bridget's hand shot up immediately.

"No way do you know the answer that fast," P.J. said.

"When you boys ran off to look at the armor and swords at the Art Institute, Sandra, Chrissy, and I went to the special showing of the ten pictures that were going to be in tonight's concert. The artist's name was Victor Hartmann, and he painted over four hundred paintings."

"I am impressed," P.J. said grudgingly. "If the last question would have been about swords or armor, I would've gotten it right."

"Thanks for buying the ice cream, P.J.," Bridget said patting her stomach.

"Shhhh…I hear instruments," Bobby said. "Let's clean up. I want to watch the players warm up."

An usher showed them to their seats that were in the center of the pavilion.

Members of the orchestra made their way onto the stage and sat down. Dale was impressed that the brass players played lip slurs and long tones.

Karl leaned over and said, "They're doing the same thing we do to warm up."

"The woodwinds are playing arpeggios and long tones, too, so we must be warming up correctly," Chrissy said.

"Can you believe that the percussionists actually practice crashing cymbals? I need to learn how they do that," Dave said.

The students watched until the lights flashed. "How come the lights flashed?" Tommy said. "Are we going to lose power?"

A man in front of their row turned around and said, "That's just a signal that the concert is about to start and people should move to their seats."

"We ought to tell Mr. Jeffrey about that for our concerts," Bobby said.

The lights dimmed and the audience applauded as the conductor, Pierre Monteux, dressed in a white tux and carrying a baton strode onto the stage. The orchestra members stamped their feet.

"We also do that ... just like the Chicago Symphony," P.J. said proudly.

At the end of the opening overture, the crowd erupted in applause with some of the audience members shouting, "Bravo!" The applause faded and before the symphony began, Bridget leaned forward and whispered, "This piece has three movements, so don't clap between the movements." The group nodded in reply, remembering that Mr. Jeffrey said that clapping between the movements destroys the flow of the piece.

At intermission, they left their seats in the pavilion to go to the ice cream stand. As part of the bet, P.J. treated them to ice cream.

Chrissy took a big lick of her ice cream. "I hope someday I can play with that kind of emotion."

"How can they play so many notes and not make any mistakes?" Bridget said in amazement.

The lights flashed signaling that it was time to return to their seats. The second half began with the stage empty except for a string quartet that would perform Tchaikovsky's *Andante Cantabile.* Following the quartet, the orchestra returned to play the final piece, *Pictures at an Exhibition,* by Modeste Mussorgsky.

As the last note echoed through the rafters of the pavilion, the audience jumped to its feet giving the Chicago Symphony a standing ovation.

P.J. elbowed Dale. "Where's Bridget going?" The boys watched as she made her way down the aisle to the front of the stage. When the applause stopped and the musicians stood to leave, Bridget reached forward on the stage and pulled on the conductor's pant leg.

Surprised, the conductor whirled around and looked down. Bridget said, "Mr. Monteux, that was the most amazing performance I've ever heard. Would you autograph my program?"

Kneeling on the stage, the conductor took the pen from Bridget. "What's your name, young lady?"

"Bridget Nielson, sir."

He wrote, "To Bridget Nielson, the next generation of musicians." Leaning down to hand the program to Bridget, he took her hand and kissed it. "A great pleasure to meet you, Bridget," he said and he stood and walked off the stage.

When she returned to her row, she held out her hand to Chrissy, and said, "It was on my list."

"To get kissed on the hand?"

"No...to *Do something spontaneous*. This counts don't you think?"

"It sure does. I'm going to get the flute section to sign my program," Chrissy said. Dale moved toward the front just as the trumpet section was leaving. He waved his program to get their attention. "Excuse me, my name is Dale Kingston. You're the greatest trumpet players I've ever heard. Would you sign my program?"

The four trumpet players looked at each other and approached Dale. "Thanks for the compliment. Do you play trumpet?" the lead player said as he came forward.

"I play cornet now, but can't wait to get a trumpet when I join the orchestra in high school."

"I think we all started on cornet before moving to trumpet. My name is Renold Schilke," the tall man said, "and this is Geralk Juffman, Frank Holz and the young man next to him is Edward Masacek. We'd love to sign your program. What's your name again?"

"Dale, Dale Kingston from Libertyville, Indiana, sir."

Each of the trumpet players signed Dale's program and shook his hand before walking off stage. Mr. Schilke was the last to sign. "Libertyville... I was there doing some competitive pistol shooting at the Sportsman's Club last November. Everyone was talking about a young man that saved the town from a fire by playing his bugle. You wouldn't happen to be that young man would you?"

Dale nodded. "Yes sir, but now I'm learning the cornet."

"It's an honor to meet you. Maybe the next time I have a competition in your area, you could come out and shoot with me. Perhaps we could throw in a cornet lesson as well," he said, his eyes twinkling.

"That would be swell. I didn't know that musicians were also involved in sports."

"Sure we are. Just because you play an instrument doesn't mean that's the only thing you do."

Dave ran up behind Dale and tapped him on the shoulder. "We don't want to miss the train!"

"Thanks, Mr. Schilke," Dale called as he ran to the back of the pavilion where the group was waiting.

Mrs. Simpson led the way through the crowd to the train. As they approached the platform, she turned and counted heads. "Wait, I only count nine." In the distance, the horn of the approaching train sounded.

Bridget said, "Where's P.J.? I thought he was right behind me."

The train glided to a stop. The conductor got off and announced, "All passengers for train number 163 to Chicago and stops in between should board at this time. Please have your tickets ready." The conductor helped the passengers up the steps into the train.

"We can't leave without him," Bridget said, her voice getting louder and higher.

"Why don't you get on," Mrs. Simpson said calmly. "The conductor will make one more announcement before the train leaves. We still have a few minutes, so I'll find him," and she left running back toward the pavilion as they climbed the steps into the train. Once on board, they found some seats together. Dale sat down and pressed his face to the glass, searching for P.J.

When the last few passengers were boarding, the conductor stood on the platform and looked both ways. "This is the final boarding announcement for train number 163. A-L-L ABOARD."

He signaled for the engineer to leave and began to climb the steps onto the train when they saw Mrs. Simpson, P.J. and a tall dark-haired man running toward the train, waving their arms and shouting.

The conductor held out his hand and pulled P.J. up into the train just as it started to move. Mrs. Simpson and the dark-haired man waved as they tried to catch their breath.

P.J., his shirt hanging out and sweat running down his face, wobbled his way down the aisle to where the group was sitting.

Bridget stood and punched him in the shoulder, hard. "Where were you?" she demanded.

P.J. flopped into an open seat. "That was some run from the pavilion." After he regained his breath, he said, "I saw everyone getting autographs and thought I wanted to get one from the tuba players. I didn't see them on stage, so I searched the backstage area. I found them and they signed my program. Then, I heard the train whistle. One of the tuba players, Arnold Jacobs, ran with me to make sure I made the train. We ran into Mrs. Simpson, and the three of us ran as fast as we could. I could see you looking out the windows of the train. You all looked scared."

"Scared?" Bridget said, her voice rising in anger. "Can you imagine what trouble we'd be in if we'd lost you?"

Dale interrupted. "From now on we stay close. Agreed?"

"Agreed," P.J. said.

The interurban train stopped every few minutes and a steady stream of people departed. Finally they were the last people in the car.

Sandra looked around. "How come no one's left? I don't see many lights on the streets. Did we miss our stop?"

Dale shook his head. "Don't worry. We were told to go back to the same station we left from."

Tommy agreed with Sandra. "There aren't a lot of people around."

The conductor passed through the car. "Next station Merchandise Mart, next station Merchandise Mart."

"Excuse me, sir." Dale said. "Will there be cabs at this stop?"

"Not on this side of the tracks. All the cabs are on the other side of the street. Just go down the steps and you'll find a tunnel that goes under the tracks."

When the train came to a stop, the doors opened to a dimly lit station.

"Where are all the people?" Tommy said.

"Stay together so we'll feel safer," Dale said as the group went down the long stairway and headed toward the tunnel.

"Listen...did you hear that?" Chrissy said.

"Hear what?" Bridget said holding tightly to Chrissy's hand.

"It sounds like footsteps. I think someone else is in the tunnel."

"Don't be silly, girls," Tommy said. But, then he stopped

short and listened. "It does sound like someone's coming." They ran to the end of the tunnel.

"Let's get in a tight circle with the girls on the inside and wait until we see who it is," Dale said.

As they stood close together, P.J. said, "No one would attack a group of ten, would they?"

"What do you mean attack?" Bridget said edging closer to Sandra and Chrissy.

They stood silently as the footsteps came closer. Finally a man in a black trench coat and hat emerged from the tunnel. When he saw them, he opened his arms.

"What took you kids so long? Mr. and Mrs. Capitanini sent me to pick you up. I didn't see anyone, so I went looking for you," Anthony said.

Bridget burst out of the center of the group and hugged Anthony. "We weren't sure who was coming down the tunnel. We were scared to death."

Anthony laughed. "I must admit you did look a bit frightened standing in a little group."

"I wasn't." P.J. said.

"Yeah right, Mr. tough guy. You were as scared as us and you know it," Bobby said.

"Let's get out of here. This place is giving me the creeps."

Anthony led the way to the car. It took about ten minutes to get to Union Station.

"Go through those doors and down the steps to the lower level. You'll see a big signboard with all of the trains listed.

Find your train number and the track your train is on. Hurry, you have about twelve minutes."

"Thanks, Anthony! Be sure you thank Mr. and Mrs. Capitanini for us," Dale said.

They piled out of the car, staying close together, and ran down the stairs. As they got to the signboard, they heard an announcement. "All passengers for train 2203 to Libertyville and all stations in between should all board at this time on track number twenty seven."

"Let's run," P.J. said as he turned to run.

"Wait, that's just the first announcement. We have plenty of time to get on the train. It isn't until they say, 'This is the final boarding' followed by 'A-L-L ABOARD' that the train leaves," Tommy said.

"Sorry, I'm just a little jumpy about missing trains."

Mr. Paulson was waiting on the platform as they arrived at the track. "I count ten bodies, so your trip must have been a success. Climb aboard car number one that is behind the engine and tender. I have seats reserved for you. I'll come by later to hear about your adventures."

The group made their way down the track to the first car, talking and laughing all the way. It wasn't until they plopped down on the large cushioned seats that they realized how tired they were. Before the train left the station, they were all fast asleep except Dale and Chrissy who were sitting next to each other.

"I had no idea when you suggested we take a trip to Chicago it would be so exciting," Chrissy said as she took Dale's hand in hers.

Dale squeezed her hand, and he felt her head fall on his shoulder. Pulling a blanket Mr. Paulson had left for each of them over her shoulders, he whispered, "I can't think of anyone I would rather have spent the day with."

Dale felt a hand on his shoulder. "I think I'll have to wait to hear about your adventure some other time," Mr. Paulson said.

"It's been a great day. Too bad it has to end so soon," Dale said.

"Their trip may be over, but not yours," Mr. Paulson said. "Follow me."

Chapter 28

UNEXPECTED FIRST

Dale carefully moved Chrissy's head off his shoulder before following Mr. Paulson toward the front of the car.

"Where are we going? What do you mean my trip isn't over yet?"

"We need to hurry before the train leaves the station," and Mr. Paulson opened the door and helped Dale climb down onto the platform. They scurried toward the large black steam engine. Dale looked up at the cab of the locomotive. The engineer who wore a hat and goggles with a handkerchief over his face leaned out of the driver's window and waved.

"What are we doing here?"

"Why don't you ask him?" Mr. Paulson said pointing to the engineer who was climbing down the ladder from the cab. He jumped to the ground and removed the red handkerchief and goggles.

"Grandpa!" Dale said giving him a bear hug.

His grandfather slapped him on the back. "I saw your list of the twelve things you wanted to do this summer and noticed that one of them was to ride in a locomotive. I arranged my work schedule so I would be the engineer on tonight's train. I want you to ride with me in the cab. I kept it a secret from everyone, including your mom and grandmother. I had to pull a few strings with my boss, but he finally gave me permission."

"I can't believe it!"

"Now climb up the ladder so we can leave on time." Grandpa turned to Mr. Paulson. "Once we get to Libertyville, have Dale's friends come up to the engine. They'll certainly get a kick out of seeing Dale in the cab."

"Gotcha, C.H. Enjoy your ride. You'll remember it forever."

As Dale climbed into the cab, he was met by the fireman that was responsible for keeping the fire stoked in the boiler. He, too, had on goggles with a handkerchief over his face, just like his grandfather.

Dale stuck out his hand. "Hi, I'm Dale." The fireman pulled down his handkerchief and lifted his goggles.

"Call me Rosy," he said shaking Dale's hand. "I've been your grandfather's fireman for over twenty years. He's the best there is."

He handed Dale some overalls. "Put these on over your clothes so they don't get dirty from the coal dust. You'll also need to wear these goggles, hat and a kerchief. These locomotives are hot, dirty and noisy machines. Since we ride with the windows open, they're pretty windy, too."

Dale pulled on the overalls, tied the kerchief over his mouth, and put the hat and goggles on while grandfather and Rosy readied the locomotive for the trip.

"Dale, sit here and look out of the window until we're out of the station and get the train up to speed. After that, I'll explain how these incredible machines work. Someday these steam engines will all be replaced by diesel engines. Tonight you're not only able to complete one of your firsts, but also you're able to ride in one of the few remaining steam engines."

Grandfather showed Dale a chain hanging from the ceiling of the cab. "Time to go. Pull this chain twice for about one second each time."

Dale reached up and pulled the chain. The loud whistle startled him as it echoed inside the station. A puff of steam came out at the same time. Dale watched as his grandfather fidgeted with the many knobs and levers. Rosy had the iron door to the furnace open and was shoveling coal in so the boiler would heat the water. The hot water made the steam that the engine used to power the wheels. Gradually the massive engine began to move, making a chugging sound that got faster and faster as the train gained speed.

"What do you think so far?" Grandpa shouted over the roar of the engine.

"It's swell, but how do you steer the train?"

Both men laughed. "You don't steer an engine. The train runs on rails and the wheels can't slip off. Each wheel has one side that has an edge on the inside and keeps the wheel on the track. All we do is slow the train down or speed it up. It follows the rails. Here, let me show you."

For the next four hours, Dale helped shovel coal and blow the whistle at crossings. Because the engine boiler was in front of the cab, he had to lean out the window to see the track ahead. He now understood why they wore the goggles and kerchiefs with all the smoke, dust and dirt flying around the cab.

"How fast are we going?"

"Right now, about eighty miles per hour, but she can go as fast as one hundred and twenty. We have to follow the signs along the track that tell us the speeds we can run at. We also have to slow down in towns and on sharp curves so we don't tip over. On some of the straight sections of track, we'll take her up to over a hundred miles per hour. In fact we're coming to one section ahead. Let's put some more coal in the fire box, get the steam up and run her up to a hundred," grandpa said as he turned several valves and levers to release more steam to the pistons that drove the wheels.

The train was traveling at about eighty miles an hour, and in no time, they were up to one hundred. Dale stuck his head out the window and looked down at the shiny rails that glistened in the moonlight. The wind blasted his face as they rumbled down the track. Dale's heart was racing with the thrill of flying through the countryside.

"I'm going to be rather busy as we approach Libertyville, Dale, so sit over here and enjoy the ride. I'll explain everything I'm doing so you can see that running a steam engine is no easy job." Grandfather explained how he slowed the train down by controlling the amount of steam to the wheels. Dale could see the lights of Libertyville twinkling in the distance. He couldn't believe the trip was almost over.

As the lights of the town grew brighter, the train continued to slow. The loud chugging sound returned along with the clouds of steam and smoke from the engine. Once the train entered the station, Dale could see a large group of people waiting on the platform.

"Are those people waiting to get on?"

"Probably not. I think it's your friends' parents who are anxious to make sure you're all safe and sound." Grandpa leaned out the window. "I see your mom and grandmother. Hang on and stick your head out the door and wave to them. We'll surprise them after we stop when you take off this equipment and they can see who you are."

Dale leaned out and waved at the waiting parents. At first they just stood there. Finally, a few waved back, but they were puzzled why an engineer would be waving at them through the door. When the train stopped and all the passengers got off, Dale watched as his friends stepped off the train and into the arms of their parents. His mom and grandmother were talking to his friends and looking around. Then he saw Mr. Paulson speak to the group, and they moved toward the engine.

"Dale, sit on my seat in the driver's window. When they get up next to the engine, blow the horn twice like you did before. Then you can take off your goggles and kerchief and wave at them from the cab."

"OK, blow it now!"

Dale pulled the chain twice and two shrill whistles sounded, causing the group to put their hands over their ears. Dale pulled off his goggles and kerchief and leaned out the door waving. The group just stood there staring up at him.

"Surprise! It's me."

"Dale, is that you? We can't recognize you with all that grime on your face," his mom said.

Grandpa came to the door of the cab and put his arm around Dale's shoulder. "He's one first-class engineer!"

"Dale, get down from there and give us a hug. We've been worried sick about you all day," grandma said. "The both of you are going to need a scrubbing with my castile soap!"

Dale climbed down the ladder and was surrounded by his friends.

"All I have to say is that this has been a great *Summer of Firsts* so far. Let's go home...I'm exhausted."

Chapter 29

ENDINGS — BEGINNINGS

The cool breeze felt good on Dale's face as he finished his third run up Simpson Hill. It had been two days since the group had returned from their trip to Chicago. Dale slept almost all day Sunday, only waking to eat and share some of the experiences with his family. On Monday when Dale was not playing with Scout or practicing his cornet, he spent the rest of his time lying on the living room rug in front of the radio listening to news of the war that seemed to be coming to an end.

Dale finished his run and did his sit-ups and chin-ups. He looked forward to meeting the gang at the fire station so they could listen to the latest war news while they sat around drinking colas, reminiscing about their trip to Chicago.

Summer vacation was winding down, and they would soon be starting junior high. Dale dropped from the chin-up bar, as he thought about the new school year. It was August 14, and school would start in about two weeks.

"Come on, Scout. Let's water the garden and see how those pumpkins and watermelons are doing. We should be about ready to eat those melons. The pumpkins have about another month before they're ready to pick." Scout barked twice and took off toward the garden. As Dale picked up the hose and turned on the water, he heard Scout barking frantically. He rounded the corner of the garage to the garden where Scout was running up and down the rows growling.

"Quiet down! What has you all…" Dale stopped in mid-sentence when he saw the garden. All but two of his watermelons and pumpkins from his Victory Garden that he had planted in April and carefully tended were smashed. Orange pieces of pumpkin rind were scattered down the rows. The pulp spattered against the ground. Ripped-up vines were tossed to the side haphazardly. Dale stood speechless as Scout growled and looked down the alley.

"Dale, would you tell Scout to stop barking. He's going to wake the entire neighborhood," mom said from the back door.

Dale motioned to his mother to come to the garden. "Look at what happened!"

Dale's mother called grandmother to join her and both of them were soon standing with their arms around Dale shaking their heads.

"Who would do this kind of thing? I've had a garden here for over twenty years and never have I had anyone vandalize it. But, what I don't understand is that they destroyed only the pumpkins and watermelons. The tomatoes and other vegetables are untouched," grandmother said. "It's as if they only wanted to ruin your part of the garden."

Mother surveyed the damage. "I don't know what to say. I know how hard you've worked to get this garden to grow. Do you have any idea who would do this?"

Dale didn't answer, but he had a hunch. Only one person caused Scout to bark and growl and only one person would do something mean like this. Dale could feel his temper rising.

"Dale, did you hear your mother?" grandmother said.

"I'm sorry, I was just thinking. No, I can't think of anyone who would do this," Dale said not wanting to alarm them. He knew what would happen if he told who he thought did it. Mom, grandma, and grandpa would go to Jim's house and confront him and his parents. He also knew he would deny it, and he didn't want his parents fighting his fights. He would tell them if he needed to later, but for now, he would pretend not to know until he could prove it.

Grandma was furious. "If I find out who did this, I'll call officer O'Malley and put them in jail."

"Let's go inside, Dale," his mother said. "There's nothing more we can do."

"At least I still have two watermelons left."

"You always seem to find the silver lining, don't you?"

"Why focus on something I can't change? Dad taught me that. That reminds me, I need to eat breakfast and hurry down to the fire station. If the war ends, dad will be home for good!"

"There you go again, seeing the positive in everything," and his mother put her arm around him as they walked back to the house.

"Come on, Scout! Let's go." But, Scout just sat in the ruined garden looking down the alley, ignoring Dale.

"That dog sure is on alert. What do you think that's about?"

"It must be his training from the military that has him guarding the garden and perhaps me."

"Why should he be guarding you?" Mom said, looking carefully at Dale.

"Oh, I meant he's guarding the garden, not me."

During breakfast Dale steered the conversation away from the garden and to the talk of the war ending. He didn't want his mother's or grandparent's suspicions aroused. After excusing himself, he packed his rucksack for the day, and whistled for Scout who was still sitting at the garden.

"Scout, come!"

Scout took one last look down the alley and ran to catch up with Dale who was going out of the driveway. As he rode by Chrissy's house, she yelled out her window on the second floor.

"Where are you riding to so fast?"

"I'm headed to the fire station to listen to the radio. We're hoping the war ends today."

"Me, too! If it does, there's talk of a big celebration on the square."

"Let's meet there if it does happen."

Dale rode down Simpson Hill. "You know, Scout, I'm thinking too much. I need to have some fun today. What do you say?"

Scout barked twice in reply. When Dale got to the fire station, the rest of the gang was deep in conversation. Mr. Walsh had the radio hooked up to speakers so they could hear the radio both inside and outside the station.

Dale slid to a stop in front of P.J.

"That radio is really loud. We can play outside and listen to the radio at the same time," Dale said as he jumped off his bike. "Let's pick teams. I need a good game of baseball to clear my head."

"Clear your head of what?" Victor said picking up the bat and ball and returning to the back of the firehouse.

"I'll explain later."

The rest of the day was spent playing ball or cards in the shade during a break between games. The radio announcer kept giving updates about the possible surrender of Japan. At around four o'clock, the broadcaster said that President Truman would talk to the nation at six o'clock. Dale was having so much fun playing that he hadn't thought about the garden or the bully until they were sitting on the benches outside the fire station sipping a cola.

Victor said, "What was that comment about this morning? The one about you needing to clear your head?"

"It's not like you to be so serious. What's up?" Tommy said.

Dale lowered his voice. "If I tell you, you'll have to promise not to tell anyone. Not your other friends, parents, and even the girls. It's a secret between us, swear."

"We swear not to tell," Bobby said crossing his heart.

The boys listened quietly to Dale as he told the story about the garden, Scout treeing Jim and his friends several weeks earlier, and how Scout seemed to sense something was wrong.

"We're behind you the whole way. When someone messes with one of us, they mess with all of us. We're just like the three musketeers movie we saw last week, *One for all and all for one*," Dave said raising his arm in the air like the musketeers had done in the movie.

All of the boys raised their arms together, forming a pyramid. "All for one and one for all!"

"I'm glad I can count on you."

"You're our best friend. We won't let you down," P.J. said slapping Dale on the back. "Now let's cook some hot dogs. We'll take them up on the roof and listen to the radio while we eat."

Mr. Walsh had built a fire pit for the boys so they could roast the hot dogs on sticks. After getting another cola from the machine, they took their hot dogs up on the roof.

"I sure like sitting up here. You can see the whole town and can feel the breeze better up here," Karl said.

From below they could hear the radio announcer say, "We now interrupt the regularly scheduled program for a special announcement from President Truman." Then the program changed to a live broadcast from the White House. "Good evening, America. I have received this afternoon a message from the Japanese government of the unconditional surrender of Japan." As the President continued to speak, the boys heard horns honking in the distance. Overhead a firework exploded, and then without warning, the firehouse siren shrieked above them causing them to put their hands over their ears.

Victor stood up and pointed toward the square and mouthed some words that the boys could not understand. They looked to where he was pointing. People streamed into the streets and swarmed into the town square. From the roof of the station, it looked like a stream of ants was attacking the square. The town was beginning the celebration of the end of the war.

Tommy leaned over the roof and shouted as did the other boys. From below, Mr. Walsh motioned for them to come down. The boys couldn't understand what he was saying, but they raced to the second floor and slid down the pole to see the fire truck pulling out of the station. P.J. led them as they climbed into the back of the fire truck. This would be a real celebration and not the subdued one that took place at the end of the European war in May.

"Hang on boys! It's time to celebrate!" Mr. Walsh said as the fire truck took off with the siren blaring. The boys in the back waved and shouted to the crowd that was converging on the town square. The fire truck edged by Sergeant O'Malley who had given up trying to direct traffic through the main intersection of town. He just stood helplessly by his squad car as people began leaving their cars in the street, and going to the square. The fire truck arrived at the square and pulled over. The shops that were normally open were closed and people were hugging, kissing, yelling, and dancing by the hundreds. The boys climbed off the truck and waded into the crowd, enjoying the celebration.

"Head to the band stand," Karl said. "We can climb the trees for a better view." The boys worked their way toward the trees with Dale falling a little bit behind the group. Before he knew it, he was by himself in a sea of people, celebrating the end of the war. He couldn't see which tree the boys had climbed. He stood still and scanned the trees above him. He felt someone bump into him. It was Sandra who burst through the crowd and into his arms. She gave him a huge hug and a kiss at the same time. Releasing Dale, she shouted over the crowd, "My list is finished," before turning and disappearing back into the crowd.

Dale stood stunned having been hugged and kissed by Sandra. But, before he could recover his composure, Bridget burst from the crowd and lunged into Dale's arms, giving him a hug and a kiss just like Sandra. Stepping back she said, "Well, my list is finished!" She then disappeared into the crowd.

Dale was confused by the two sudden hugs and kisses. He looked upward to search the trees for his friends when he felt a tap on his shoulder. As he turned around, he was met by Chrissy who fell into his arms and gave him a kiss on the lips. She stepped back and smiled. "Now my list is complete," she said as she ran back into the crowd.

Dale was a little stunned and stood in the middle of the crowd. He felt another tap, one that was a bit harder than Chrissy's. This time when he turned, he came face-to-face with Jim Petris and his friends.

"Can't find your friends, big shot? And, I don't see that tough dog here to protect you either," he said moving his face closer to Dale's. "What's the problem, Mr. I Saved the Town? No one here to save you?"

Dale stood his ground, unwilling to show his fear. He didn't know if he should fight or run, but his anger was rapidly rising and his neck and face were bright red, which caught Jim momentarily off guard. Just when Jim took another step closer, Tommy, Victor, Karl, and Dave dropped down from the trees above. They had been perched in the branches above, watching Dale as he was being kissed by the girls. P.J. and

Bobby came pushing through the crowd, sweating and out of breath, to join the other boys.

Jim backed up when the boys dropped from the trees. Dale said, "Sorry, Jim, but did you say something about me being alone?"

"Don't worry, Kingston. Your time will come when you come to the junior high and band," Jim said as he began to walk away.

"And by the way, how are those pumpkins and watermelons you've been growing?" Over the noise from the crowd, Dale could hear his evil laugh as he joined his friends and melted into the celebration.

Dale patted Victor and Karl on the back. "Thanks, guys! I can't believe you dropped down just in the nick of time."

"We climbed the tree right next to where you were standing. You thought we went on, but we were just above you. You couldn't hear us shouting at you because of the crowd noise," P.J. said tucking his shirt in.

"We saw the entire thing, starting with the girls hugging and kissing you. What was that about?" Victor said. Dale was as confused about it as they were, but he was flattered and especially amazed by Chrissy.

"When we saw Petris and his cronies working their way through the crowd, we knew we had to act fast. You should have seen the look on that bully's face."

"One for all and all for one!" Tommy said. The boys raised their arms in the air signifying unity.

"Come on let's celebrate the end of the war. Maybe I'll get kissed and hugged," P.J. said.

Dale laughed on the outside, but he said to himself. *"So he's the one who trashed my garden. I'm not going to let a bully push me around. I'm going to have to step up and confront this problem myself."*

About the Authors

Paul Kimpton grew up in a musical family and was a band director in Illinois for thirty-four years. His father Dale was a high school band director and later a professor at the University of Illinois, and his mother Barbara was a vocalist. When Paul is not writing, he is reading or enjoying the outdoors.

Ann Kimpton played French horn through college and went on to be a mother, teacher, and high school administrator. Her parents, Henry and Maryalyce Kaczkowski, both educators, instilled an appreciation of the fine arts and the outdoors in all of their children.

Ann and Paul were high school sweethearts who met when they played in the high school band. They have two grown children, Inga and Aaron, who share their love of music, the outdoors, and adventure. They now have two grandchildren, Henry and Teagan, who, no doubt, will continue the tradition.